FAR SCAPE™

HOUSE OF CARDS

FARSCAPE™

HOUSE OF CARDS

Keith R. A. DeCandido

TOR®

A TOM DOHERTY ASSOCIATES BOOK
NEW YORK

This is a work of fiction. All the characters and events portrayed in this book are either products of the author's imagination or are used fictitiously.

FARSCAPE: HOUSE OF CARDS

A Tor Book
Published by Tom Doherty Associates, LLC
175 Fifth Avenue
New York, NY 10010

www.tor.com

Tor® is a registeed trademark of Tom Doherty Associates, LLC.

ISBN: 0-812-56162-7

First edition: May 2001

Printed in the United States of America

0 9 8 7 6 5 4 3 2 1

Dedicated to the fond memory of Jim Henson.

From seeing Kermit the Frog reporting from the planet Koosbane as a child to being thrilled by the lush alien landscapes of Farscape *as an adult, my life has been enriched by Henson and his great legacy.*

Now's my chance to give something back, however small.

ACKNOWLEDGMENTS

Primary thanks have to go to all the folks responsible for making *Farscape* into the wonderful show it is, from the magnificent actors, to the talented producers, to the brilliant writers and directors, to the glorious Henson puppeteers. Bravo to all!

Huge amounts of thanks go to my editor, Guillaume Mutsaars of Boxtree, and to David Mack and Craig Engler of SciFi.com.

I got a great deal of help from a variety of reference sources: the official *Farscape* web sites maintained by SciFi.com (www.scifi.com/farscape), Henson Productions (www.farscape.com), and the BBC (www.bbc.co.uk/farscape); the excellent "*Farscape* Fantasy" web site run by "Dallascaper" (www.farscapefantasy.com—and be sure to say hi to Geoffrey the Giraffe!); and the reference book *Farscape: The Illustrated Companion* by Paul Simpson and David Hughes.

Large thanks also to my bandmates in the Don't Quit Your Day Job Players (for being patient with me), the Forebearance (who made me the Muppet I am today), Marina Frants, the Geek Patrol, Laura Anne Gilman ("Bear left!" "Right, frog"), Glenn and Brandy Hauman (who were a big help in the development of Liantac), the Malibu gang, John J. Ordover, Terri Osborne (whose editorial assistance went *way* above and beyond), Marco Palmieri, and all the loonies on SciFi.com's *Farscape* BBoard and PsiPhi.org's *Farscape* discussion board. Also thanks to the web sites Charlie-Yardbird-Parker.com and www.legendsofmusic.com/Elvis Presley for invaluable aid.

But the most thanks of all have to go to Greg Cox at

Tor Books. From Iron Man to *Gargantua* to Spider-Man to *Star Trek* to the X-Men and the Avengers to *Farscape*, we've been through lotsa licences together. Here's to the latest.

AUTHOR'S NOTE: *House of Cards* takes place towards the end of the second season of *Farscape*, between the episodes "Won't Get Fooled Again" and "The Locket."

CHAPTER 1

Rygel flipped his cards over. "Four priestesses. I win again."

John Crichton snarled, threw his cards on the table, and got up out of his chair. "Enough. I'm gonna owe you my module at this rate."

The Hynerian's tiny form quivered with laughter. "Only if you put it in the pot. Though don't think I don't appreciate all the food cubes you've lost to me." Rotating his flying ThroneSled ninety degrees, he popped one of those cubes into his oversized mouth.

Shaking his head, Crichton sighed. "Yeah, I'm sure they'll last you at least a few minutes."

Rygel started shuffling the twenty-eight-card deck. "Care for another chance at winning your cubes back?"

"Remind me, Sparky," Crichton said as he sat back down, "why did I let you talk me into learning this game?"

"Because Haunan doesn't work with only one player, and no one else on this ship has even come close to comprehending it. Zhaan refuses to gamble, D'Argo couldn't seem to wrap his poor Luxan brain around the rules, and Aeryn wouldn't even sit down with me to learn it."

"What about Chiana?"

The wisps of white hair that jutted from Rygel's cheeks twitched as he shuffled, but he said nothing.

Crichton smiled. "Wait, let me guess—she beat the pants off you? Or she would have, if you wore pants."

"I prefer an opponent who stimulates me," Rygel retorted, with a haughty sniff. "And while Chiana has many virtues—"

"You're only 'stimulated' by winning, right?" Crichton tossed a food cube into the middle of the table as an ante. "Fine, Maverick, one more hand. Deal."

The deposed dominar of the Hynerian Empire dealt a card face down to both Crichton and himself. Crichton peeked at the card, and saw that it was a paladin, which meant it was all but useless.

Haunan was an odd game. Rygel had been after Crichton to learn it for some months, and Crichton had finally broken down earlier in the day, out of boredom as much as anything. It was just similar enough to poker for Crichton to be able to follow the basics. You get six cards, of which you can use four; you're dealt two cards, one up, one down, and then you bet; repeat that process until you have six cards, three showing that everyone can see, three down that only you can see; and the highest hand wins. It was just different enough from anything Crichton had ever seen to confuse the hell out of him and give him the mother of all headaches.

Still, it wasn't like he had anything better to do. Moya, their sentient, bio-mechanoid Leviathan ship, was resting between StarBursts in this uninhabited star system. Crichton had done as much maintenance on the *Farscape I* module as he could with the materials at hand. The rest of Moya's crew were busy with other occupations or duties.

That left Crichton in the unusual position of hanging out with Rygel.

When John Crichton found himself on the Leviathan after his space shuttle, *Farscape I*, had torn through a wormhole and zipped him halfway across the galaxy, he'd become a member of a very strange crew. Though Pa'u Zotoh Zhaan and Ka D'Argo were both convicted murderers, Rygel XVI, a "mere" political exile, was the hardest to warm to. Whatever crimes they may or may not have committed, they had all been incarcerated by the Peacekeepers—who were sort of a combination of the Mafia, the Green Berets, and Genghis Khan's army. Even Moya, the Leviathan, had been enslaved by the Peacekeepers as a prisoner transport ship.

Rygel had been the one who broke all three of them out of their cells. Soon thereafter they had removed the control collar that the Peacekeepers had placed on Moya and freed her as well. They'd been on the run ever since, hiding in the Uncharted Territories, theoretically out of the Peacekeepers' jurisdiction. However, they'd learned the hard way over the two cycles since then that the Peacekeepers had a very fluid idea of what constituted their jurisdiction.

Crichton often suspected that the only reason why the arrogant, obnoxious Hynerian—who rarely had anything practical to contribute—hadn't met with the business end of an airlock early on was out of gratitude.

Still, Rygel had had his uses. His political and gambling skills had saved their bacon on more than one occasion. Even his size had proven useful. Once when only his small hands could reach a Peacekeeper device that needed to be removed. And another time when his rear end plugged a hole in Moya's inner hull, saving Crichton and Chiana from explosive decompression.

And, truth be known, Crichton did feel sorry for the little guy. A firefight with an alien ship had led to Crichton's mind briefly inhabiting Rygel's body, and it had not been a pleasurable experience. Everything burbled or gurgled or emitted a noxious odor, and those tiny Hynerian arms and legs were even more impractical than they looked—which Crichton hadn't thought possible until that moment. The whole experience had been a lot like walking around in a sewer. *After six hundred cycles trapped in that bod,* Crichton had thought at the time, *I'd be a whiny bastard, too.*

As Rygel dealt Crichton a queen, D'Argo's deep, resonant voice sounded over the comm. *"John, can you come to the Command?"*

"What's up, D'Argo?"

"It looks like we have a visitor. Pilot's picked up a trading ship heading right for us."

"We're in the ass end of nowhere," Crichton replied. "It's the Uncharted Territories' equivalent of South Dakota. What the hell's a trading ship doing here?"

"That's why we want you up here," D'Argo said patiently. *"Zhaan and Aeryn are on their way up as well."*

"Rygel and I'll be right there."

There was a pause. *"Fine."*

Crichton couldn't help but chuckle. D'Argo probably hadn't realized that Rygel was with Crichton, and the Luxan obviously wasn't thrilled with the Hynerian being present. But then, D'Argo was never happy when Rygel was around.

In fact, it was rare that D'Argo was happy, period.

Crichton hurried from the cargo bay, where he and Rygel had been playing Haunan, to the Command, Rygel's ThroneSled right behind him. All the corridors on Moya essentially looked the same—it had taken Crichton months just to nail down the routes to and from his quarters. And even after all this time, there were still parts of the ship he wasn't completely familiar with. However, the parts he knew, he could navigate in his sleep.

Zhaan and Aeryn entered the Command from the corridor opposite Crichton and Rygel. D'Argo and Chiana were already present. A small holographic image of Pilot was visible in one corner, piped in from his den.

On the big viewscreen in front was a small ship. It didn't look like much of anything, but ships rarely did from the outside.

Pilot's gentle voice sounded over the speakers. *"They*

identify themselves as a free trader. They have minimal weaponry, which is not presently armed."

Minimal weaponry was still more than Moya had. The sum total of the Leviathan's tactical systems was a balky defense screen salvaged from a Peacekeeper hulk. "Have you answered them yet, Pilot?" Crichton asked.

"No. We were waiting to hear from all of you. Moya is concerned, but she cannot StarBurst for another half an arn, and that ship is faster than we are."

Zhaan looked at the others with her trademark serene gaze. Crichton always wondered how much of that was the Delvian's many centuries as a priest and how much was simply the overwhelming blue of her eyes against her equally blue skin. "I believe we should listen to what they have to say," she said.

"Me, too," Crichton chimed in quickly, grateful that at least one other person would take his side. Especially as he expected either Aeryn or D'Argo to disagree.

"Absolutely not," the two of them stated, in perfect unison. Crichton sighed.

Like Crichton, Aeryn Sun had been brought on board Moya during the prisoners' escape from the Peacekeepers. The irony was, Aeryn had been one of the officers assigned to stop them. Her contact with Crichton, D'Argo, Zhaan and Rygel had led to her being declared contaminated by alien influence—a capital crime among the Peacekeepers. Rather than face a death sentence, she had remained on Moya, and had become a valued part of the team in general.

And a very important person to John Crichton in particular.

Chiana spoke up. "Well, we don't have anything to lose by talking to them." She was leaning on one of the consoles, her slate-grey skin and matching outfit standing out against the dull browns and golds of the console. She wasn't quite standing up straight. Then again, Chiana always seemed to stand at about a twenty-degree angle to the rest of the universe—both literally and morally.

"They're hailing us again," Pilot said. *"They say that they have been searching for a Leviathan for some time."*

"Look, they're a trading ship," Rygel said. "If they need a Leviathan specifically, it's probably for something that they'd be willing to pay us for."

D'Argo snarled. "Money *would* be the first thing *you* think of."

"Pip's right," Crichton said, agreeing with Chiana. "We don't have anything to lose by talking to them."

"Fine," Aeryn conceded, "I'm willing to *talk*."

Crichton looked at D'Argo, who simply snarled again.

"I'll take that as a yes. Pilot, open a channel."

Times like this, Crichton thought, *I wish I could make like Captain Picard and say that we come in peace*. Sadly, reality didn't work like that. They met precious few people out here who had peaceful intentions. *And the ones who do usually want to screw us over some other way*, he reflected.

The face that appeared on the viewscreen belonged to a Luxan. Crichton blinked in surprise. He hadn't expected to encounter another member of D'Argo's race—certainly not running a trade ship. This man had less facial hair than D'Argo—just a small moustache that reminded Crichton of one of his high-school math teachers—and of course, he did not have the tattoo on his chin that D'Argo wore as a result of the latter's one-time impersonation of a general. Otherwise, though, he had the characteristic flat nose, articulated eyeridges, bald head, and weird back-of-the-head tentacles of the Luxan race.

"I am Bu G'Ranto of the trading ship Qualik. *I have a passenger on board who's been looking for a biological ship. Your Leviathan seems to qualify."*

"I'm Commander John Crichton. What is it your passenger wants?"

G'Ranto looked at D'Argo. *"This Sebacean speaks for your ship, General?"*

D'Argo hesitated. He had never been comfortable with the fact that he had once impersonated his commanding officer in order to save him from torture, nor with the fact that the mark of a general was now permanently displayed on his chin. For that matter, Crichton himself wasn't always comfortable with the fact that people assumed he was a Sebacean. But what else would they assume? Sebaceans—the race that formed the Peacekeepers—outwardly looked just like humans.

"We all speak for the ship," D'Argo said. "Crichton's words are mine."

"If you say so. In any case, what he wants is safe passage to a world called Liantac."

Rygel floated up next to Crichton and laughed. "No one has gotten 'safe' passage to Liantac for thirty cycles."

"That is no longer the case, Hynerian," G'Ranto responded, looking at Rygel as if he were a fly in his soup.

I guess D'Argo isn't the only Luxan whose butt Rygel gets up, Crichton thought with a smile.

G'Ranto continued: *"The atmospheric catastrophe that prevents ships from entering Liantac's orbit only prevents inorganic propulsion systems from functioning. Apparently, biological ones work just fine. According to my passenger—whose name is Rari, incidentally—the locals have constructed techno-organic vessels that ferry people to and from the planet. Unfortunately, none of them come out this far, and I can't afford to divert my vessel all the way to where the ferries go. But your ship can go right to the planet. Apparently it's his home, and he hasn't been there for over a cycle. He's willing to pay a considerable sum for passage."*

"Define 'considerable', " Rygel said.

"We'll get back to you within the arn," Aeryn interrupted. "Screen off, Pilot."

G'Ranto's face faded, leaving only the view of his ship.

"I don't think we should go," Aeryn said.

"I very much think we should," Rygel said with a far-away look in his eyes that Crichton hadn't seen since the last time Rygel had had a gourmet meal. "I've been dreaming of going to Liantac for ages!"

"It's a dren-pit, and we shouldn't go anywhere near it," Aeryn said.

Rolling his eyes, Crichton said, "Will someone please provide some closed-captioning for the Uncharted Territories–impaired?"

Rygel took up the challenge. "Liantac is the home of the most glorious place in all the known galaxy: the Casino."

Crichton blinked. "Casino?"

D'Argo nodded his head. "A gambling planet."

"Not just '*a* gambling planet'," Rygel said with all the haughtiness he could muster—which was a considerable amount. "*The* gambling planet. I had thought that it was off-limits after what happened thirty cycles ago, but if biological ships can approach. . . ."

Aeryn shook her head. "It's also on the fringes of the Uncharted Territories—dangerously close to Peacekeeper-controlled space. We shouldn't risk getting that close without good reason."

"I think restocking supplies is a good reason," Rygel argued. "Liantac was always a good supply port, from all accounts. And we're being *paid*."

"Sparky's got a point," Crichton conceded. "The pantry's gettin' kinda bare. We could use a shopping spree, and something to spend on it. Hell, Aeryn, you're the one who's been bitching about needing spare parts for your Prowler."

"I am also running low on some of my medicinal herbs and other drugs," Zhaan announced. "I think we should take this Rari up on his offer."

"So do I," Crichton said.

"Me, too," added Chiana.

"I believe I've made my position clear," Rygel said.

D'Argo sighed. "Much as I hate to say it—I can't think of a good reason why we shouldn't."

"*I* can," Aeryn said. "Every time we've come near Peacekeeper space, something's gone badly wrong. For that matter, every time we've taken on passengers, something's gone badly wrong."

Chiana actually straightened up at that. "Hang on, you took *me* on as a passenger."

Aeryn smiled a nasty smile. "My point exactly."

"Look," Crichton said, "the guy just wants to go home. We can get him there. Now, I don't know about the rest of you, but I think that it would be the right thing to do to help him out."

"John is right," Zhaan said. "We have all been taken from our homes. It would be . . . fitting if we could facilitate someone else being able to return to his."

"*Especially* since they're paying us," Rygel added.

Pilot spoke up. *"I've received another communiqué from the trading ship. They can provide specific course and StarBurst information that will allow us to get within a few light years of Liantac. And—Moya agrees with those that say we should do this. She feels that the potential benefits outweigh Officer Sun's concerns."*

Aeryn fixed Crichton with a look. "I'm not going to convince any of you, am I?"

Grinning, Crichton replied, "Not without firearms."

"Fine. Let's do it, then."

Crichton turned to the screen. "Bring G'Ranto back up, Pilot."

The Luxan's face reappeared, and he looked straight at D'Argo. *"Have you decided, General?"*

Crichton frowned. *And frell you, too, Chuckles*, he thought.

D'Argo replied, "Yes. We will take Rari aboard and off your hands."

"Assuming," Rygel said quickly, "that the price is right."

Still looking at D'Argo, G'Ranto said, *"Will five hundred retri be sufficient for the purposes, General?"*

"It will be—" D'Argo started, but Rygel interrupted.

"That will not be even remotely sufficient. We must receive at least a thousand for going so far out of our way."

Now G'Ranto did acknowledge Rygel. *"You have a Leviathan, Hynerian. You can StarBurst. No place is 'out of your way'."*

"Then I'm sure you can find someone who will act as a ferry for such a paltry sum. Good luck in that endeavour." Rygel moved forward as if to cut the connection.

Crichton tensed. He hoped Rygel hadn't just blown the deal. He also wondered just how much a retri was worth.

"Wait," G'Ranto said. *"Seven hundred retri."*

Breaking into a wide grin, Rygel said, "Very well. I assume Rari will bring the payment when he arrives. We will, of course, expect the full amount in advance."

"Of course," the Luxan said disdainfully, then turned back to D'Argo with a more respectful look on his face. *"It was a pleasure meeting you, General—?"*

"And you as well," D'Argo said, ignoring the implied request for a name. "Let us know when you're ready to send him over. Screen off."

G'Ranto's face once again faded.

"Excellent!" Rygel said. "I haven't had a good game of Tadek in far too long. In fact, the last time I played, I had to deliberately lose to that yotz, Kcrackic."

"Well, I'm sure you'll have plenty of opportunities to lose legitimately, Rygel," Aeryn retorted, leaving the Command in what could only be described as a huff.

Crichton sighed.

"According to the signal I'm receiving from Bu G'Ranto," said Pilot, *"a shuttle from his ship will be approaching within half an arn. By the time it arrives, docks, and provides us with the coordinates, Moya should be ready to StarBurst."*

"Great," Crichton said. "Let me know when he arrives, I'll go meet him."

"I'll join you," Zhaan said.

Aeryn stood in the corridor, fuming and waiting for D'Argo to leave the Command. To her relief, he came out alone, making it that much easier to confront him. As he turned a corner out of sight of the Command, she stepped in front of him. "What the frell has gotten into you, D'Argo?"

"What do you mean?"

Imitating D'Argo's deep voice, Aeryn said, " 'Much as I hate to say it—I can't think of a good reason why we shouldn't.' There are dozens of reasons why we shouldn't be taking this trip, and I would've thought *you*, of all the crew, would be on my side in pointing them out!"

"Maybe," D'Argo said. "But I thought that Crichton and Zhaan's arguments were good ones. For that matter, so was Rygel's. We're getting paid for this, and we can put that to good use."

"Assuming Rygel doesn't lose it all at his frelling card games," Aeryn muttered.

Smiling a small but vicious smile, D'Argo said, "I'll make sure that won't be an issue."

Aeryn returned the smile. She sometimes wondered why they didn't just shove the Hynerian out of an airlock.

D'Argo continued: "But we're also helping someone get home, and I can't say that I don't feel for him."

Aeryn rolled her eyes. "Don't tell me you've bought into Crichton's heroic nonsense?"

"No," D'Argo admitted. Then he looked right at Aeryn— and beneath his fierce Luxan exterior, Aeryn saw a look of genuine longing in his brown eyes. "But sometimes I'd like to."

"Really?" Aeryn said with more than a little dubiousness.

"Yes, really," D'Argo said defensively. "And I'm not the only one."

"What's that supposed to mean?"

"Whether we're willing to admit it or not, Aeryn, Crichton *has* rubbed off on us, at least a little."

"Don't be so sure of that."

"Really? Then why haven't you turned us all in? A good Peacekeeper—" and D'Argo snarled the word "—would do her duty regardless of the consequences. A hero does the *right thing* regardless of the consequences. What have you been doing more and more these past two cycles?"

Aeryn found herself unable to answer the question.

"You see my point," D'Argo continued after Aeryn had been silent for several microts. "We're not soldiers anymore, Aeryn—either of us. If I've learned nothing else from Crichton—and from Chiana, and, damn the little dren-sucker, even Rygel—it's that we can't be what we once were ever again. Which means we need a new way to be. Why not a better way?"

"Sounds more like you've been listening to Zhaan too much," Aeryn muttered.

D'Argo laughed. "Perhaps. But it's worth thinking about—even for people like us who don't like to think."

With that, D'Argo continued on his way down the corridor.

Aeryn sighed. The fact of the matter was, she not only knew that D'Argo was speaking the truth, but she had had this same conversation with herself more than once since first meeting John Crichton and being convinced to stay on Moya rather than face Peacekeeper "justice" for being contaminated by aliens.

And she had changed, obviously. But had she changed enough? Or was she just fooling herself?

She headed towards her quarters, more confused than ever.

CHAPTER 2

"Y ou guys go ahead and shop till you drop," said Crichton. "I'll stay on Moya."

Aeryn stared at Crichton for several microts. "I don't believe I heard you correctly. It *sounded* like you said you were staying on Moya."

"Yup. That's what I said," Crichton replied, grinning.

"Crichton, you *never* stay on Moya if you don't have to. Usually you can't get off the ship fast enough."

They were standing in the hangar, preparing Moya's transport pod for travel. Since it, like Moya, was organic technology, it was able to function in Liantac's otherwise untraversable atmosphere. Aeryn's Peacekeeper Prowler— the ship she'd been issued with during her tenure with the Pleisar Regiment—and Crichton's module would be useless on this trip.

Aeryn was absolutely right, of course. Crichton doubted that the others would ever truly understand why he was always so eager to go on-planet wherever they went—after all, they were born into societies where interplanetary travel

was as common as crossing the street back home. But for
Crichton, a man who'd always dreamt of navigating the
stars while growing up on a world that could barely get its
act together for a trip to the moon, being able to step on a
new world was an experience he never wanted to pass up.

Well, hardly ever.

"Thing is, Rygel's spent the entire solar day it took to
get here quoting me chapter and verse about Liantac," he
explained. "It sounds *way* too much like Vegas or Atlantic
City for comfort."

"I'm going to assume that, like every other incomprehensible reference you make, those are places on your
homeworld?"

Crichton nodded. "The last thing I want to do is trigger
unnecessary homesickness. So I'll just stay here."

Aeryn shrugged. "Suit yourself."

"Meanwhile," Crichton continued, handing Aeryn a list,
"if you see any of these parts lying around, I could use
them for my module."

"Fine," Aeryn said, taking the list without bothering to
look at it.

Crichton smiled. "What, no smartass comments about
why should I bother doing repairs on my silly little module
with its primitive engine?"

Fixing him with her classic don't-frell-with-me look,
Aeryn replied, "Would it do me any good?"

"Prob'ly not, no."

"There's your answer."

The door to the hangar opened, and Rygel, Chiana, and
Zhaan entered, followed by their new passenger. Like all
Lians, Rari was bipedal, but apparently descended from
avian rather than simian stock. He had dark feathers on his
head, there was vestigial plumage on other body parts that
on a human or Sebacean would be hair, his arms were fairly
long relative to his height, and his legs were disproportion-
ately short. And he had a beak instead of a nose and mouth.

That beak made talking to him interesting, as he couldn't
make any sound that involved the pressing of two lips to-

gether—B, F, M, and P sounds were a lost cause. This gave rise to a brief source of confusion when Crichton had to explain that he was not a "Selacean."

"I'd like to thank you all again for taking me home," Rari told Moya's crew.

Zhaan gave Rari a small smile. "There is no need to thank us, Rari. The seven hundred retri you paid us shows your gratitude."

The retri—which only came in coins—was the currency of Liantac and, from what Rygel had said to Crichton, it was good on many other worlds as well. Given that the coins were made of precious metals—gold, silver and something the others called "nelg"—most folks would probably take them as currency of some kind or other. The money was to be split evenly among the crew—a hundred each for the seven of them, including Pilot, whose share would go towards supplies for Moya, since he had no real material needs beyond caring for the Leviathan.

"Still, I am grateful. And I think you'll find my home-world a very hospitable place."

"I'm counting on it," Rygel said with a laugh.

Chiana's mouth couldn't decide whether to smile or sneer. "I think it's safe to say that Rygel's hundred retri will work its way back into the Liantac economy very quickly."

"Hah!" Rygel said. "You'll be chuckling out of the other side of your mouth when I've accumulated enough wealth to buy this planet."

"Can we please go?" Aeryn asked, almost pleading.

"Yes, we should," Rari said, looking at Aeryn and Zhaan. "I can direct you both to the places you'll need to go for the items you seek."

"Thank you," Zhaan said.

Within a few microts, the five of them had boarded the pod. Crichton left the hangar so that Aeryn could complete the departure sequence—which included exposing the hangar to space.

Part of Crichton thought that he should have gone planetside. True, it might have triggered homesickness—on the other hand, it might have been therapeutic. *No*, he decided. *It's not worth the risk*. Twice, Crichton had been put into scenarios intended to make him believe he'd made it home. He would not put himself in that position again, even in such an indirect way as going to a place similar to Vegas.

And from the way Rygel described it, it was fairly similar, down to the entertainment. The image of an overweight Elvis Presley playing to a room full of aliens suddenly came into Crichton's head, bringing a smile to his face. *I can just see the King crooning "Viva Las Vegas" to a bunch of drunken bird-people* . . . He moved into a clumsy approximation of the classic Elvis pose and started crooning, "Viva Las Vegas! Vi-i-i-i-iva Las Vegas! Thenkyew. Thenkyew verra much."

Then he looked quickly around to make sure that there were no DRDs nearby. The Diagnostic Repair Drones performed various physical functions onboard Moya on Pilot's behalf, and they weren't actually sentient, but Crichton would've still been embarrassed to have one of them see his performance.

Now, unfortunately, the tune to "Viva Las Vegas" was running through Crichton's head. Normally, when unwanted songs invaded his consciousness, he'd be able to mentally cleanse himself with something from Charlie Parker's oeuvre—usually the solo from "Ornithology."

That, sadly, didn't seem to be working this time. No matter how hard he tried, the Yardbird's trademark saxophone sound always modulated into the King crooning about Vegas.

Bird, my man, you're failin' me, Crichton thought.

So he gave in, and started singing "Viva Las Vegas" as he went to the Command.

Or tried to.

By the time he made it to the Command, he had tried several times to dredge the lyrics up, but he couldn't remember anything aside from the "Viva Las Vegas!" refrain at the end of each verse.

"What nonsense are you uttering?" D'Argo asked as Crichton entered.

"It's a song. It's called 'Viva Las Vegas'," Crichton told the Luxan, singing the title Elvis-style.

D'Argo snorted. "Your definition of 'song' is obviously much more liberal than mine."

With a bark of laughter, Crichton said, "Don't go pulling the musical high ground with me, pal. I've heard you make noise on that shilquen of yours."

Pilot came over the comm, *"The transport pod is safely entering the atmosphere. The high levels of larik particles are having no impact on the pod."*

"The whozits particles are what's keeping inorganic ships from working, right, Pilot?" Crichton asked.

"Yes."

"Cool. Keep us posted if anything goes wrong." He turned back to D'Argo. "Anyhow, I can't get this song out of my head." Crichton then proceeded to "sing" the entire first verse, after a fashion—it was more of a hum, really, since he substituted "da" for each syllable until he got to "Viva Las Vegas!"

"I see," D'Argo said. "You can't get it out of your head, so you're determined to get it into mine. At least Luxan songs have words."

"So does this," Crichton said, exasperated, "but I can't *remember* them. And I can't exactly call up www.elvis.com and look 'em up. So I'm stuck." He sat down. "Okay, maybe if I take this slowly, line by line."

"John."

Closing his eyes and ignoring D'Argo, Crichton spoke aloud to himself: "Try to visualize that time you saw that garage band cover it. No, that won't work, you couldn't understand a word they said. Think, John, *think*."

"John," D'Argo said again.

"Let's see, first line has something about a city in it."

"John!"

"What?" Crichton finally answered, opening his eyes and turning to D'Argo.

"If you *insist* on trying to remember that idiotic tune, do it somewhere else."

"But—"

"I'll call you if something happens."

"Some pal you are," Crichton muttered as he got up. "Can't you at least take pity on me in my hour of need?"

"I'd rather you took pity on me and not give *me* an hour of need," D'Argo retorted, with a menacing smile.

"Fine," Crichton said, heading towards his quarters. "Catch you later, dude."

At least D'Argo was smiling, Crichton thought. *A cycle ago, he'd have shouted me out of the Command at the top of his lungs while holding his Qualta at my throat, instead of gently with a smile.*

Crichton stopped in his tracks. *A cycle ago. When did I stop thinking in terms of years?* He shook his head. *Probably around the same time that I forgot the lyrics to "Viva Las Vegas."*

Sighing, he continued to his quarters, trying to reconstruct the first line beyond the word "city."

Chiana first saw the lights from orbit.

The pod made one orbital pass, then began its descent. The bonosphere was choked with larik particles, but the lights—which, based on what Rari and Rygel said, were from the Casino—penetrated even that gloom, to some extent.

Once they descended into the lower atmosphere, Chiana got a better view of the planet. Most of what they saw consisted of fairly uninteresting plains broken up by an occasional body of water.

Then the Casino came into view.

At first, Chiana could only see the glow. Holograms, signs, decorations, bright lights, all in shimmering, vibrating colors. As they came closer, she could start to make out details. Some of them advertised products. Some of them displayed the name of the establishment. Some listed featured attractions. The big holographic signs were obviously for the fanciest places, but Chiana was most impressed with the two-dimensional signs that still managed to look striking—doing the best they could with what they had. Chiana admired that.

The common theme was that all of them were selling *something*. Chiana had the feeling she was going to like this place.

It took her several microts to notice that the signs were all attached to one large building.

Actually, the word "large" didn't do it justice. The Casino was apparently one massive complex that dwarfed Moya in size. *In fact*, Chiana thought, *you could get three or four Moyas in there*. All the different establishments—gambling places, restaurants, bars, entertainment centers, the stores that Aeryn and Zhaan intended to visit, and everything else—were located inside this one huge structure.

"Ah, I've missed this place," Rari sighed. "It's good to be home."

Chiana shrugged. Of all those on Moya, she was the only one who had no desire to go home—she had been an outcast on Nebari, having had the temerity to think for herself—so she didn't share the others' feelings of homesickness.

She did, however, share Rygel's desire to explore this planet. It looked like a fun place. Especially for a girl with a hundred retri in her pocket . . .

A small holographic image of a female Lian with her yellow feathers done up in what Chiana thought was a hideous pattern appeared in front of Aeryn. *"Greetings, and welcome to Liantac, the greatest planet in the galaxy! You are not on our scheduled manifest. Please identify yourself so we can expedite your arrival and service here on Liantac."*

Chiana shuddered. The relentlessly cheery voice reminded her a little too much of her fellow Nebari after they'd been mind-cleansed—a fate Chiana had been earmarked for before she'd been rescued by Crichton and the others.

"We're from a civilian ship," Aeryn replied. "We're transporting a local named Rari."

"Please wait a moment," the hologram said. Then: *"DNA scan verifies the presence of Citizen Rari. Welcome home, Rari! We hope you will remain home for a long time to come."*

"Thank you," Rari said warmly. "That is my intention."

Chiana rolled her eyes. Rari sounded as fake as the hologram. There was something about him that had rubbed Chiana the wrong way from the moment he came over from the Luxan trader. She wasn't sure how much of it was Rari and how much was her own distrust of someone whose face she couldn't easily read—facial expression cues that one had with Nebari and other races weren't there with the beaked Lians. Even so, there was a certain insincerity that Chiana got from Rari that she didn't like in someone other than herself.

"Excellent," the hologram said. *"DNA scan identifies the rest of you as a female Sebacean, a female Delvian, a female Nebari, and a male Hynerian. Will you be visiting the Casino?"*

"Yes," Aeryn said, and Chiana noticed the disgust in the Sebacean's voice.

A display with some kind of navigational data that Chiana found completely incomprehensible appeared next to the image of the woman. *"Please follow this route to Hangar Bay 72. From there, attendants will direct you to a dock that can accommodate your pod."*

"Thank you," Aeryn said. "Go away now, please."

"Upon your arrival, you will be given free—"

"I said, *go away!*" Aeryn repeated. "We've identified ourselves and I have the information I need to land. You've served your function. Go away."

Without losing the cheery tone, the hologram said, *"I don't see any need to take that tone. We're only trying to provide you with the best service possible here on Liantac, the greatest planet in the galaxy!"*

Chiana tried and failed to contain a giggle at the look on Aeryn's face. The ex-Peacekeeper looked as though she wanted to strangle the hologram—Chiana knew the look well, having been on the receiving end of it more than once.

The hologram droned on about the gifts they'd receive and recommended various places to go. Aeryn finally landed the pod at the outer edges of the Casino in an area marked with a large numeral 72, and sure enough, a male Lian directed them to a slot in the bay.

"Enjoy your stay here on Liantac, the greatest planet in the galaxy!" the hologram told them, before finally winking out.

"I knew we shouldn't have come here," Aeryn muttered as she exited the pod.

"Oh, come on, Aeryn," Chiana said, "lighten up. They just want to make sure that we have a good time here."

"I'm not here to have a good time."

Rygel exited the pod. "Well, *I* am. The next time you see me, I'll be disgustingly wealthy."

"Halfway there already," Aeryn muttered.

Zhaan smiled. "Come, Aeryn. Let us go and do what we need to do."

Nodding, Aeryn said, "The sooner the better. We'll meet back here in twelve arns."

"Twelve arns?" Rygel said imperiously. "That's not nearly enough time!"

"Put it this way, Rygel—in twelve arns, this pod goes back to Moya with or without you. Clear?"

Rygel's ears drooped. "As clear as Luxan blood."

With that, the Hynerian steered his ThroneSled towards the exit.

Chiana smiled. "Well, *I'm* going to check out some of those drinking establishments."

"Mind if I join you?" Rari asked. "I can show you

some of the finer taverns—not the ones the tourists go to, but the *good* ones."

At first, Chiana was going to say no. But for the first time, she got a sense of sincerity from Rari. *Interesting*, she thought. *And worth exploring.*

She smiled. "If you can keep up with me, you're welcome to come along."

From the beginning, Aeryn Sun had wanted nothing to do with Liantac, and the planet itself had done nothing to convince her otherwise.

She wasn't sure what annoyed her most, the garishness of the decor or the obsequious cheer of every native she encountered, from the hologram that invaded the pod to the attendant at the hangar bay. The latter had gleefully announced that parking privileges cost a quarter retri per arn, with a minimum of four arns, those first four arns payable up front. Sighing, Aeryn paid one retri out of Moya's share, then she and the Delvian followed the signs to the northern end of the Casino, which was where Rari had said the best merchants were.

Perhaps it's not the garishness or the false cheer, but the frelling noise, she thought as they walked down the concourse. Aeryn had spent all of her life onboard ships, where things were orderly. Even in the turmoil aboard Moya, there was still a certain structure, a certain quietude. But here, everything bombarded her. It was as if she were surrounded by a wall of sound. Even the noisiest taverns she'd been in were quieter than this.

Everyone around them seemed to be in a ridiculous hurry. They ran eagerly into the gambling places, or the restaurants, or the entertainment halls—as if they were in a rush to part with their money.

That was probably what disgusted Aeryn the most. Everything here was designed to separate visitors from their cash as quickly and efficiently as possible—and the visitors seemed eager to take part in the process. She'd seen that eagerness in Chiana and Rygel on Moya, and now in almost every single being around her. Aeryn shook her head. *I will never understand this. And I will never understand why we came here.*

"It seems that we must take this monorail," Zhaan said, pointing to a sign to that effect.

"Fine, let's go."

The monorail cost another quarter retri each. The person who took the fare said, "Thank you so much for riding the Liantac Monorail, the best monorail on the best planet in the galaxy!"

Somehow, Aeryn managed not to punch him.

They stood on the platform, waiting for the next monorail to show up. Aeryn had thought they would be among the few aliens present, but the platform seemed evenly split between Lians and offworlders. *Obviously those ferries do decent business,* she thought, though from what she knew of Liantac before the catastrophe, the percentage of offworlders used to be a good deal higher. Even so, there were a good number of non-Lians, ranging from Sebaceans to Luxans to Sheyangs to Vorcarians to Ilanics to Halosians. She even saw an occasional Nebari—*probably outcasts like Chiana,* she thought. *I can't imagine their oppressive society approving of their citizens coming to a place like this.*

A Lian female walked up to the two of them. She held a pile of small chips engraved with an ornate logo. "Would you two like some free passes to the Harilear Club?" she asked, holding out two of the chips. "We have a special tonight for any offworlders—first two drinks on the house. And Licit will be performing two shows every night."

"No, thank you," Zhaan said with a polite smile.

The Lian moved closer to Zhaan. "I really think you'd like it. Licit is the most popular singer on the planet, and we've got some fantastic—"

"She said *no,*" Aeryn said, moving between the Lian and Zhaan.

"You don't understand, this offer is only—"

"No, *you* don't understand. You have five microts to

move away from me before I remove your feathers with a dull blade."

The Lian's eyes went very wide. Then, after a pause, she moved on to irritate someone else.

Zhaan grinned. "Nicely handled."

"Yes, well, you have to know how to reason with these people."

A monorail pulled in.

"Welcome to the Liantac Monorail, the greatest monorail on the greatest planet in the galaxy, which is brought to you today by Ornara's Emporium, home of the finest Haunan tables on Liantac."

As they boarded, Zhaan said, "Well, I'm sure Rygel will wind up there, ere long."

"Think it'll take him all twelve arns to lose the hundred retri?"

"Don't be so sure. I saw him when he deliberately lost at Tadek to Kcrackic. Rygel does have some skills."

"Most insects do."

The monorail had a dozen or so rows of bench-like seats facing front. Each wall was covered with an advertisement of some sort, which changed every ten microts. Aeryn dutifully ignored them all.

Well, nearly all. The one on the front wall was a bit harder to ignore, as it had an audio component and was staring her straight in the face. Presently, holograms of two Lian males, dressed in outfits that rivalled the signs outside the Casino for garishness, began to speak.

"Hello there! I'm Willby!"

"And I'm Yaren."

"We're the proprietors of—"

"Willby and Yaren," they chorused.

Willby continued solo: *"You can fulfill your every pleasure at Willby and Yaren."*

"That's right. Whatever your fantasy, whatever your enjoyment, you can find it at Willby and Yaren, or your money back."

"That's a guarantee—we promise to give you pleasure no matter what it is."

"And if you don't get it, you'll get a full refund of your entry fare, plus free drinks all night long."

"There's a thought," Zhaan said.

"What?"

"You could go there."

Aeryn looked at Zhaan as if she'd started budding again. "You can't possibly be serious."

"Why not? They guarantee your greatest pleasure. Why not go in there and say your greatest pleasure would be to blow up the planet?"

In spite of herself, Aeryn had to laugh.

"Actually, that's not a bad idea."

"The worst that can happen is that you get your money back and free drinks," Zhaan continued.

They spent the rest of the monorail ride pointing out the stupidities in the various advertisements—a relatively easy task, and one that Aeryn found herself enjoying.

When they arrived at the stop that was closest to the merchants on the northern side, Aeryn said, "Thank you, Zhaan. I needed that laugh."

Zhaan simply gave Aeryn that enigmatic smile of hers. "My pleasure." She looked around. "Rari said that the herb merchants are this way, and the used parts emporium he recommended is that way. Should we arrange to meet somewhere, or simply rendezvous at the pod in eleven-and-a-half arns?"

"Let's just meet back there. I don't know how long this will take—though, honestly, I'm not holding out much hope. If this place hasn't had any ships by in thirty cycles, I can't imagine they have anything useful."

"Perhaps not," Zhaan said, "but it's worth looking."

"Definitely. Parts of the Prowler are being held together with little more than good thoughts. In any case, I'll see you at the hangar bay."

Zhaan nodded. "Very well." And she went off in search of the herbs and medicines she required. Aeryn had no idea

what it was, exactly, the priest would be getting, but she
trusted that whatever it was would be beneficial. Zhaan's
skills as a healer had proven tremendously useful on more
than one occasion.

As Aeryn proceeded down the concourse, a Lian male
walked up to her holding a pile of chips. "Hi there! When
you're done shopping, how'd you like—?"

Aeryn glared at him.

"No, I don't suppose you would like," the Lian went on,
barely missing a beat. "My apologies." And he walked off.

First intelligent person I've met on this frelling planet,
Aeryn mused.

She almost missed the place, as it didn't have a brightly
colored sign or holographic characters imploring people to
enter. Instead, it was a simple entryway with a two-
dimensional sign in block letters. STRAN'S USED PARTS EM-
PORIUM: BUY AND SELL NEW AND USED SHIP PARTS.
REASONABLE RATES.

The entryway was through a curtain of wooden beads
hanging from the top of the doorframe. Inside was an open
space. The walls and floor were strewn haphazardly with
parts of every type of ship Aeryn had ever seen, and several
she didn't recognize.

Here, an engine part from a Peacekeeper command carrier. There, a communications array from a Sheyang transport. Over here, a command chair from an Hynerian
imperial cruiser. Next to that, weapons from a Luxan military yacht.

At the back was a desk, currently unoccupied, sitting in
front of another beaded entryway. The only unoccupied
floorspace was a narrow path that had been cleared from
the front entrance to the desk.

A voice sounded from the back: "Be right out! Feel free
to look around!"

"Thank you," Aeryn replied, happy to do so. She was
amazed at the collection of . . . *stuff*. There wasn't enough
here to make one functioning ship, but the sheer variety of
machinery was astonishing. Leaning side-by-side up against

one wall were a Scarren plasma conduit and a generic-looking connector port. Sitting on the desk were a pile of Tavlek gauntlets. Involuntarily, Aeryn shivered. She, Crichton, and D'Argo had had a bad experience with one of those drug-delivering monstrosities that heightened aggression. Aeryn never wanted to see one of those frelling things again.

There was a pile of spare engine parts in one corner, and she was about to start sorting through it when she heard the rattle of beads. A Sebacean man came out from the back room.

"Hello, I'm Eff Stran, and I—" he started as he walked out, wiping his hands with a cloth of some kind. He was fairly scruffy-looking: unkempt hair, scraggly beard. In fact, he reminded Aeryn of what Crichton looked like when he'd been trapped on Acquar.

He cut himself off when he looked up at Aeryn.

Suddenly, his face contorted under the beard and he screamed, *"Get the frell out of my store!"*

"What?"

He reached behind the desk and pulled out a pulse rifle. It was Peacekeeper issue, to Aeryn's surprise and dismay. "I said get the frell out of my store, you Peacekeeper khan!"

"There must be some mistake, I—"

"Oh, there's no mistake, Officer Sun." At the use of her name, Aeryn recoiled as if she'd been slapped. "You have five microts to get out or I'll kill you where you stand."

"Look, this must be some mistake. I've never even seen you before."

And then, in a flash of memory, she realized exactly who the store's owner was. Once she got a good look at the face under the beard and hair . . .

Technician Eff Stran. How could I have forgotten?

In a subdued voice, she said, "I'm sorry. I didn't realize that—I'm sorry," she ended, lamely.

Without another word, she turned and left, half-expecting Stran to shoot her in the back, half-disappointed that he didn't.

As she made her way back towards the monorail, Aeryn spoke into her comm. "D'Argo, can you hear me?"

After a moment, D'Argo's powerful voice sounded through the tiny speakers. *"Yes, Aeryn, go ahead."*

"I'm going to need you to take my place down here. I've run into a—problem with the store that provides spare parts."

"What kind of problem?"

"A personal one. If I take the pod back up, can you find the parts that Crichton and I need and then meet up with Zhaan?"

Aeryn heard Crichton in the background—it sounded like he was singing something. *I'm not even going to ask*, she thought.

"Under normal circumstances, I might refuse. I'm a warrior, not a purchasing agent." He paused, and then continued in a lower voice, *"But I'll be more than happy to get away from Crichton for a while."*

"Has he finally gone insane, or is this just the latest example of his usual idiocy?"

"Apparently, there is some song from his planet that he can't remember the words to. He's been trying to re-create the memory since you left. I tried to kick him out of the Command, but he keeps coming back. Remember what you said about being around Zhaan this long having an effect on me?"

Frowning, Aeryn said, "Yes?"

"Well, I suspect you're right, as it's the only way to explain why I haven't killed him yet."

Somehow Aeryn managed to smile. "Well, I should be back up there in an arn or so, and you'll only have this blotching planet to deal with."

"I'll manage. See you in an arn."

As Aeryn got back on the monorail platform, she realized that, by taking the pod out before the first four arns was up, she'd be forced to forfeit all the retri she and Zhaan had paid up front.

But since the alternative was getting shot by Stran, she

had no choice. She respected Crichton's wish not to come on-planet, and D'Argo was the only other person on board she'd trust with this sort of thing.

While she stood on the platform, a Lian male walked up to her. His speckled feathers were all standing up perfectly straight, and he wore an outfit with enough clashing colors in it to give Aeryn a headache just looking at him.

"Hi there," he said, standing much closer to Aeryn than she liked. "You know, you have the most wonderful features. I work for Dallek Enterprises—we run several of the entertainment venues here on Liantac, and you would fit in perfectly with a little 'alien goddesses' show we've got going."

" 'Alien goddesses'?" Aeryn repeated, as the monorail pulled in.

"Exactly. We've already got three Nebari and two Luxans, but a Sebacean like yourself would really *make* the show. Why, put you in a nice satin number, and—"

Aeryn punched the Lian in the side of the head. He fell to the platform, breaking some of his upright head feathers. The female life forms on the platform applauded as Aeryn boarded the monorail.

It did nothing to improve her mood.

CHAPTER 3

Dominar Rygel XVI, deposed monarch of the Hynerian Empire, sat in the House of Games, feeling something he never thought he'd feel in a gambling establishment: boredom.

After winning a few simple games at which he'd become expert in his youth—Hranto, Greltek, and Fizzbin—Rygel had moved on to Tadek. By the time he'd won his twelfth straight game, he had quintupled his original hundred-retri stake. But there was no challenge to it.

His opponents were the rankest of amateurs.

He left the Tadek tables and navigated his ThroneSled toward the exit of the House of Games. An unimaginative name, but that had been part of what had drawn Rygel here. That, plus the fact that four different people had come up to him in the space of fifty microts singing the praises of the place. Such shills were commonplace in the Casino, of course, but their sheer persistence had been enough to convince Rygel at least to stop by.

Another point in its favor was that it was prominently

listed in all the directories, but not advertised like all the others in an attempt to grab as many people as possible. Even the shills weren't indiscriminately grabbing everyone who came by—only those who looked like they had serious money to spend.

The signage at the House of Games was much more subdued than of the other gambling establishments. And the casino was just for gambling—no restaurant or bar, no staged entertainment. Better still, they provided free food, a perk that Rygel had been more than happy to take full advantage of.

Everything had indicated that this was a place for serious gamblers, not the usual sort of riffraff one found in the more touristy establishments. The food and drinks were of the highest quality provided for high-rollers, and the tables didn't appear to be rigged.

Unfortunately, all the other players only *thought* they were serious gamblers. Rygel had been fleecing yotzes like them since childhood. *I suppose*, he mused, *that the slowdown in offworld traffic during the last thirty cycles has lowered the standards. A pity.*

As he neared the door, a Lian walked up to Rygel. His head had been completely shorn of feathers, but he had an unusually distinctive beak. "Excuse me, sir, but were you planning on departing?"

Rygel stopped his ThroneSled's forward motion, and hovered at the Lian's eye level. "That depends."

"On what, sir?"

"On what you're about to do to convince me not to."

"Well, sir, we simply hate to see someone of your exalted position leave."

"Exalted position?"

"You *are* Dominar Rygel XVI of the Hynerian Empire, are you not?"

Rygel's mouth twitched. While he was flattered to be recognized, he wasn't sure that it was necessarily a good thing—especially given that his image was on several wanted beacons that had been circulating throughout the

Uncharted Territories for two cycles. "I am—though I was deposed by my idiot cousin many cycles ago."

The Lian respectfully bowed his head. "We do not concern ourselves with the vicissitudes of politics, sir. We do, however, respect the high office that you represent, and I have been given leave to offer you a place at our special Haunan table. It is in the back room. Netoros has specifically requested that you be invited to her exclusive table."

Rygel's ears raised. "Really?" *This sounds more like it. Particularly after all that practice on Crichton.* Still, he didn't wish to seem too eager. "And why would this Netoros's invitation be of any interest to me?"

"Two reasons, Dominar. One, Netoros is the owner of this establishment. Two, Netoros is a member of the Consortium. There is at present, sir, a waiting list of ten solar days to be invited to her Haunan games. However, in light of your status, you have been placed at the top of that list—if, that is, you choose to accept the invitation."

In truth, there had never been any doubt of his acceptance. The Consortium was the ruling body of Liantac, consisting of seven leading business owners. Netoros and her six compeers were as close as anyone on Liantac came to being a royal personage worthy of the Hynerian dominar.

"Lead the way," Rygel announced, maneuvering his ThroneSled back inside the casino.

"Rari!" the bartender cried as the Lian and Chiana entered Terisears's, an unassuming tavern. "Thori's beak, but it's been an age. Come in, have a drink!"

It was the fourth bar they'd been to since arriving. Chiana had wanted to visit the fancy places near the gambling establishments first. She had been attracted to the bright lights, glitz, and glamor, despite Rari's insistence that those places were just for the tourists.

After the watered-down, overpriced drinks, bad music piped in at over-loud volumes, and drunken louts from whom Chiana would have expected better flirting skills given all their practice at it, she had finally agreed to let

Rari take her to the place that he claimed was his favorite bar.

The first thing Chiana noticed was that she was the only non-Lian in the place. It dawned on her that the other three bars had been mostly filled with offworlders.

Rari approached the bar and touched the bartender's left shoulder with his right hand, and she did the same—the standard greeting among Lians. "It's good to see you again, Terisears."

The second thing Chiana noticed was the lack of bright colors—which may have made Terisears's unique on all of Liantac—and the subdued music. A pleasant piece of instrumental background music was playing, low enough to allow conversation.

This place also smelled different. The others had all made an effort to put forth the most polished face they could, resulting in an antiseptic, sterile feel. But Terisears's had all of the odors one would *expect* in a bar: alcohol, sweat, wood, more alcohol.

Chiana immediately took a liking to it.

"Where *have* you been all these cycles, anyhow?" Terisears asked Rari.

"That's a very long story."

Terisears's gaze moved to Chiana. "And is this female part of that long story?"

Laughing, Rari replied, "Only the end of it. This is Chiana, one of the beings who helped to bring me back."

Terisears put her hand on Chiana's shoulder and squeezed it. "A pleasure, Chiana."

Chiana smiled. She returned the gesture, squeezing a bit in return. Terisears's eyes widened. "The pleasure's all mine, Terisears," she purred.

Rari asked, "Can we have two sunsets, please?"

Chiana made a face. "Not another sunset, those tasted like dren."

"No, the ones in those dumps you insisted we go to tasted like dren. Terisears makes the best sunsets on Liantac. Trust me."

"You took her to another bar before mine?" Terisears said in a pouty voice as she pulled down two bowls from a shelf. "You haven't been here in more cycles than I can count, and you don't come here first. Just for that, I think you should buy the house a drink."

"Nice try, Terisears," Rari said with another laugh. "But do start my tab up again, will you?"

"Of course."

"Uh," Chiana said, back in the low voice, "any chance I can get a glass?" Besides feathers, Lians also retained from their avian ancestors the habit of eating and drinking by leaning down into a stationary source rather than bringing the food and drink to their mouths. The other bars had had bowls for the natives and proper glasses and mugs for off-worlders.

"Afraid I don't have any, Chiana," Terisears said. "You come to my place, you drink like a Lian."

"Oh, *really*?" Chiana said with a V-shaped smile. "Well, I'll just have to drink Lian-style, then."

"Good for you."

"Let's get a table, shall we?" Rari said, lightly touching Chiana's arm.

Chiana grinned. He touched her arm enough to be a gentle request, not enough to be an insistence that she stop flirting with the bartender. She liked that.

"Y'know," Chiana said as they sat on low stools at a small, square table, "you never told us the long story of how you wound up away from home."

Rari shrugged. "Nothing worth telling. I followed an opportunity offworld, it didn't work out, and it took me a while to earn enough retri to get home. When I did, I was too far from the ferry routes. Luckily, I'd heard you folks were in the area, and I found you."

Terisears came with the two bowls, each containing liquid shaded the distinctive orange, red, and violet of a sunset.

"You sure about this?" Chiana said after staring at the

bowl for several microts. "It took an arn to get the taste of the last one out of my mouth."

"Trust me," Rari said.

Remembering something Crichton had once said about how when you're roaming you should do like roaming people do—or something like that—Chiana decided to follow the Lian custom. Rather than pick the bowl up and drink as she normally would, she leaned forward and lapped up her drink.

As soon as the liquid touched her tongue, she felt a gorgeous tingling sensation, as well as a taste that was not too sweet, not too tart. All the other sunsets had tasted either sickly sweet or watery, with nothing tingly remotely involved. "This is fantastic," she said to Rari, who was also lapping from his bowl.

"I told you," he said, then sat back up. "This is the *true* Liantac—good drinks, good people, nice music."

"It is very nice music," Chiana said, leaning towards Rari.

"If you have time, you should go to the Noli Den. It's a cozy little place on the southern end of the Casino. There's a band there—they've been doing this type of music there every night for the past ten cycles. They're absolutely fantastic. I might go see them tomorrow night, actually—I wonder if they even remember me."

Chiana studied Rari's face. Rari returned the gaze, no doubt thinking that Chiana was hanging on his every word. And she was, though not just in the way he imagined.

"So," she said, "you were telling me about your trip away from home."

"I've pretty much told it," Rari said quickly. "I'm actually much more interested in your story. I mean, how does such a motley crew as you lot wind up on a Peacekeeper prison ship?"

Chiana sat up straight. "How'd you know Moya used to be a prison ship?"

Rari blinked. "I saw the cells. I'm sad to say that I've been in one or two in my life. I know one when I see one, and I saw plenty on your ship."

"Was that part of the opportunity that didn't work out?" Chiana asked, with a grin.

Laughing, Rari said, "I'm afraid so." He leaned down to take another lap of the sunset. "In any case, how did you lot come together?"

"Well, I came on board after the others, so you'd be better off asking one of them. They kind of rescued me."

"Fair enough. Still, you're not exactly what I was expecting—any of you."

"What do you mean?"

Rari paused thoughtfully. "Well, you're not exactly a typical member of your species."

Chiana leaned back and laughed. "Why do you think I don't hang out with other Nebari?"

They continued to talk for the better part of an arn. Rari was full of questions about Chiana, equally full of bizarre factoids about Liantac, and completely bereft of any practical insights into his own life.

This jibed with Chiana's suspicions, which were all but confirmed when Rari had said that Moya was a prison ship. He barely missed a beat when Chiana called him on it, and most would have taken his answer at face value—but Chiana knew from years of experience what that fraction-of-a-microt hesitation meant before he replied.

Rari was lying.

He came up with a quick response, but it wasn't enough to disguise—to Chiana, at least, who knew plenty about lying—the fact that Rari had known that Moya was a prison ship before he ever came on board.

Chiana didn't know what that portended, but she was very sure that it wasn't good.

After lapping up the last of his sunset, Rari stood up. "I'm afraid I have to be getting home. I've been putting it off, really—afraid to see how much dust the place has collected," he said with another laugh. He reached down to squeeze her shoulder. "It was truly a joy to meet you, Chiana. And please extend my warmest thanks once again to the rest of your crew for coming to my rescue."

Chiana smiled her sweetest smile at him. "Happy to do it, Rari. And maybe we'll meet again."

"I'd like that very much. Take care."

Rari said his goodbyes to Terisears and a few of the bar's other patrons, and then departed.

Chiana picked up the bowl and gulped down the rest of the sunset, only spilling about a quarter of the contents on the table. Then she headed out, also wishing everyone farewell. It was almost time to meet Aeryn and the others at the hangar bay.

She had quite a bit to tell them.

"All bets have been matched," the Haunan dealer called out. "Players, show your hands."

"Two pair, kings and queens," Rygel said, flipping over the two kings and the queen he had in the hole and placing them alongside the queen he had showing.

"Damn you, Hynerian," said Steen, the burly Lian who was the only one of the foursome left in the game with Rygel. Steen's hand consisted of three priestesses, a lesser hand.

The other two players at the table had dropped out earlier. Netoros—a striking Lian female with head feathers the same blue color as Zhaan's skin—had dropped out after the first round of betting. The fourth player, a tall Nebari male named Haffax, had stayed in a bit longer. Haffax, whose skin was as slate-grey as Chiana's, but whose short hair was a lustrous black, had remained in for all six cards, but folded immediately afterwards.

Rygel was having the time of his life. *This*, he thought, *is why I wanted to come here*. Three Haunan tables were set up, with four players at each. Since each player got six cards, only four could play with a single twenty-eight-card deck. (There were variants that used two decks and could therefore have eight players, but Rygel viewed those—as well as other variants, such as the ones that employed wild cards—as beneath his notice and not *true* Haunan.) Over the past two arns, Rygel had won another hundred and fifty retri—he won most of the hands he stayed in on, and folded early when he knew he didn't stand a chance.

"Well played, Dominar," Netoros said.

"Thank you," Rygel said politely.

The dealer collected the twelve cards and dropped them into the recycler—he had already done so with Netoros's cards, Haffax's, and the leftovers after the final deal. He then retrieved a fresh deck and unwrapped it. Rygel's winnings registered on the small screen embedded in the table in front of him, and the screen in the table's center reset itself to zero.

"New game," the dealer announced. In reply, Rygel pressed a button, placing half a retri into the pot as his ante. Haffax, Netoros, and Steen did likewise, and the center screen registered two retri.

By the time all six cards were dealt, Haffax and Steen had both dropped out; the center screen displayed one hundred retri, and was growing by the microt. Rygel had a queen and two priestesses showing—a good "up" hand. Netoros had three kings up, which seemed to be the better hand.

But Rygel's three hole cards were also queens, which meant Rygel had the second-highest possible hand: four queens. The only way Netoros could beat him was if she had the fourth king. Under normal circumstances, Rygel couldn't be sure whether or not she did, since neither Steen nor Haffax had had a king as an up card before they folded.

However, Rygel had one advantage on this hand: the dealer had slipped when dealing, and accidentally flashed one of the down cards he dealt to Steen—the fourth king. Which meant that Netoros could not possibly beat him.

So Rygel raised the pot considerably.

And Netoros did likewise.

There were no limits on raises—such things were for lesser players—and so the process went on for some time. The other two tables suspended their games so they could watch.

Steen leaned over to Haffax. "Seventy-five retri says that Netoros doesn't have the other king."

Haffax smiled. "You're on."

Rygel managed to control his reaction to that, though he silently admired Steen's greed, and put in his entire remaining stake, which included a raise of one hundred retri. He assumed that Netoros would match, thus allowing him to double his winnings. Rygel was already starting to plan his victory celebration in his mind. *Something involving scantily clad females and copious amounts of food, certainly,* he thought. *And I must be sure to rub the good Officer Sun's face in my victory. Oh yes, and D'Argo's.*

"I raise two thousand retri," Netoros announced.

Rygel gasped. He forcibly removed the visions of dancing girls and a huge bowl full of marjools from his mind and focused on the task at hand. "I don't *have* two thousand retri," he coughed.

"If you cannot meet the stakes, Dominar, you must fold. House rules."

"I'm *aware* of that," Rygel said testily.

It's a plot, he thought. *She knows she can't possibly win, and she hasn't been able to drive me out of the game with her previous raises, so she's forcing my hand—so to speak. There must be something I can do.*

Leaning back in her chair, Netoros said, "If you have something you wish to offer as a substitute for money, Dominar, that is acceptable. One of your royal possessions, perhaps?"

Rygel refrained from pointing out how pathetic his collection of "royal possessions" had become over all those cycles of imprisonment. *But I must have something of value to these people. Perhaps something on Moya that—*

And then it came to him. *Moya! True, she isn't really mine to offer, but Netoros need not know that—it's not like she can win . . .*

"I will match your raise with my ship."

Haffax snorted. "Your ship is worth two thousand retri?"

Turning on the Nebari, Rygel said haughtily, "It's worth

considerably more than that—at least on this world. My
ship is a Leviathan."

A few of the onlookers gasped and muttered in amaze-
ment.

"That's right," Rygel said. "A ship that can function in
your orbit. Think, Netoros, what you could do with such a
ship. It could salvage this world's flagging economy."

Whispers flew throughout the room. Rygel ignored them,
and looked straight at Netoros. The Lian, for her part,
looked maddeningly placid.

"Very well," Netoros said finally after a pause of several
microts. "I accept your raising of the stakes. I will match
with an additional two thousand retri."

Rygel would have been happy to call Moya a matching
bet, but he wasn't about to argue with the prospect of add-
ing an extra two thousand retri to the pot he was about to
win. "Excellent."

"All bets have been matched," the dealer announced.
"Players, show your hands."

His ears raised to their height, his wide mouth spread
into a huge grin, Rygel turned over the other three queens.
"Four queens," he said.

"Thori's beak," Steen muttered.

Netoros flipped over her three cards in succession. The
first two were paladins, and therefore useless.

The third was the fourth king.

Rygel's ears drooped.

His grin fell.

I saw it! I saw that king in Steen's hand!

Steen, for his part, looked equally shocked, as he had
had that king. But he said nothing.

"A pity," Netoros said, "that you lost your entire stake,
Dominar. Not to mention your ship. I thank you for your
patronage at our establishment, and for a most enjoyable
evening of Haunan. Now then, if you will provide us with
access to your ship, we can complete the transaction."

Rygel shifted uncomfortably in his ThroneSled. *Aeryn*

and D'Argo are going to take turns dining on my entrails, he thought unhappily. *But she cheated!*

And you know this because you *cheated,* Rygel reminded himself. *She is a member of the Consortium and the owner of the establishment. You are a fugitive and a deposed monarch. Unless Steen speaks up—and based on that look of fear on his face, he won't, curse him—it's her word against yours. Or, to put it another way, her gospel against your lies. Besides, there's no proof—the dealer's already recycled the damn cards.*

Tread very carefully, Dominar.

He coughed. "Let's—talk about this, shall we?"

"I don't want to talk about it!"

When Aeryn had disembarked from the transport pod mere microts ago, D'Argo had given her a significant look and had said, "Be careful, Aeryn. He's in full human mode."

Knowing that this meant Crichton would harass, annoy, pester, and confuse her no end, Aeryn let him know exactly where he stood with her the moment she entered the Command and saw him.

For his part, Crichton seemed to be muttering something to himself—probably that song D'Argo had warned her about.

He stopped muttering long enough to ask, "Don't want to talk about what?"

"Anything. Pilot, status?"

"All systems are reading nominal. As expected, Moya's immune system is preventing the larik particles from interfering with any ship's systems."

"Good."

"So," Crichton said after a microt, "why'd you come back up here?"

"Didn't I tell you that I don't want to talk about it?"

"What else is new? Aeryn, you *never* want to talk about anything. You keep everything bottled up so tight that one of these days you're gonna explode."

Aeryn whirled on him. "Then the sensible thing for you to do would be to stay out of my way, or get hit by the shrapnel."

Crichton threw up his hands. "All right, fine."

"Fine," Aeryn repeated. She went over to one of the consoles and checked over the systems.

Or, at least, she tried to. Crichton kept singing something in a low voice off in the corner.

"Crichton, can you please go and be an idiot somewhere else?"

"I'm not being an idiot, I'm trying to remember something from home."

Aeryn looked at him with an expression of befuddlement—something she often did in his presence. "It's just a song."

"Not just any song—a song by the King!"

Sighing, Aeryn turned back to the console. She guessed that Crichton would attach importance to something by royalty. "Then do it quietly."

"Sorry, no can do. I can only reconstruct this if I sing it out loud."

Closing her eyes, Aeryn asked, in a strained voice, "Can't you do this in your quarters?"

"Tried that. The acoustics are all wrong. Echoes were driving me crazy."

"So," Aeryn said, turning back to face him, "you decided to drive *me* crazy instead?"

Grinning, Crichton got up from where he was sitting and walked over to her. "Well, there is *one* way to get me to stop."

"And what would that be?"

"Tell me what happened on Liantac."

"*Nothing* happened on Liantac. Now will you leave me alone?"

Pressing an imaginary button, Crichton said, "Bzzt! Wrong answer. You've had a bug up your ass since before you walked off that pod, and you wouldn't have cut the trip short if nothing happened. Try again."

Turning back to the console, Aeryn repeated, "I don't want to talk about it," knowing full well that it wouldn't deter Crichton.

"Tough noogies. Dammit, Aeryn, I want to help you."

Aeryn closed her eyes and exhaled. This was what angered her most of all. If Crichton's pestering was out of malice or stupidity, she could just dismiss him and deal with him the same way she dealt with other things that irritated her: intimidation or small-arms fire.

But, damn his eyes, he only asked because he cared about her.

Maybe if I ignore him, he'll go away, she thought, knowing the idea was ludicrous. Crichton had an impressive stubborn streak that was matched only by Aeryn's own. Still and all, she gazed down at the console, convincing herself that it was the only thing in the room.

"Fine," Crichton said after Aeryn didn't speak for several microts. "Viva Las Vegas!" he sang. "Vi-i-i-i-va Las Vegas! Vi-i-i-i-i-i-i-i-i-i-i-i-i-i-i-va Las Vegas!"

"Crichton!" Aeryn cried out in exasperation, turning back towards him.

Crichton cut off a fourth "Viva," and looked at her with that annoying grin of his. "Yes?"

"Don't make me have to kill you."

"Sorry, but those are the only words I know. Been trying to remember more—best I can do is something about a city on fire, but I can't quite place it."

"Can't you just forget about it? It's a part of your past, just let it go! Remembering it will just remind you of what you don't have anymore. None of us can afford to do that, or we'll go mad. So kindly shut up and leave me the frell alone!"

Crichton, looking completely unmoved by Aeryn's tirade, stared straight back at her. His blue eyes felt to Aeryn as though they were penetrating into her very soul. *Damn you, John, how do you do that? How do you get inside me just by looking at me?* It was the characteristic of the human that she both loved and hated the most. Right now she was hard pressed to choose which of the two emotions she felt more.

"There was a Sebacean on the planet," she began finally. "His name is Stran and he runs the used parts emporium that Rari recommended. It's quite an impressive place— D'Argo should be able to find everything both of us need to—"

"So what about this Stran?" Crichton said, getting her back on track.

You did it again, she thought.

"A Sebacean. A Peacekeeper. *Former* Peacekeeper." She walked over to one of the seats. "He was a tech—an engineer, I think. I don't remember, exactly."

Crichton sat down next to her. "Go on," he prompted.

Aeryn took a deep breath. "A few cycles ago, a Peacekeeper regiment rebelled against their commander. Actually, they rebelled against the Peacekeeper establishment altogether. The Fantir Regiment had led several successful campaigns against the Scarren and they were considered heroes. We were suspicious of them for a while, felt that they were becoming too powerful, but we didn't have any proof, and their status made it hard to accuse them of anything directly."

"Friends in high places?"

Nodding, Aeryn said, "Exactly. My regiment was assigned to investigate. By the time we gathered the proof we needed, Fantir had taken over a command carrier, which had to be destroyed."

"What does this have to do with the guy running 'Sanford and Son' down on Liantac?"

"A tech was doing repair work for them—unauthorized, obviously. The thing is, he didn't know what Fantir was planning to do, he didn't even know the work was unauthorized, he just followed the orders of his superiors. The Fantir officers were using him."

"Let me guess . . ."

Again, Aeryn nodded. "The Peacekeepers didn't see it that way. As far as they were concerned, he was aiding and abetting treason." For the first time since she started her story, she looked at Crichton. "I was the one who turned him in. It's funny, I didn't think he'd be allowed to live— not that I gave it any thought at the time, of course. But I suppose Fantir still had its supporters, so Stran was probably quietly exiled instead of publicly executed."

"You didn't know?"

She shrugged. "I'd done my duty and moved on to the next assignment. I didn't give Eff Stran or the Fantir Regiment another thought, until—" She hesitated.

"Until you saw Stran running a shop on Liantac?"

She stood up and walked back towards the console. "In any case, now you know, all right?"

Crichton, naturally, got up and followed her. "No, it's not all right, Aeryn. Look, you have to—"

Whirling around to face him, she shot back, "I don't *have* to do anything! I know you feel the need to muck about inside my head, but I—"

"*Officer Sun, Commander Crichton,*" Pilot broke in. "*I'm sorry to interrupt, but Moya has detected a field of some sort surrounding the planet. It's being generated by a pair of techno-organic ships that entered orbit a hundred microts ago.*"

"What kind of field?" Aeryn asked.

"*It appears to be primarily made of Clorium.*"

Crichton looked at Aeryn. "Oh, that's very not good."

Clorium was one of six elements that Leviathans were forbidden to carry, as it acted as an anesthetic to them. Moya's crew had used some once when they needed to remove a Peacekeeper beacon that had been attached to the ship's nervous system.

Aeryn looked down at the scan Pilot was doing of the field that was being generated. "If this continues at the present rate, the field will encircle the planet. That amount of Clorium would completely numb Moya and prevent her from functioning." She looked up at Crichton. "Someone doesn't want us to leave orbit."

"Apparently not," Crichton said grimly.

"*Moya is frightened,*" Pilot said.

"Yeah, well," Crichton said, "I'm not exactly Joe Cool, either. See if you can find any holes in the field, Pilot."

"*I'm searching now, but it seems to be complete. One of the ships is hailing us. They are requesting that all hands disembark immediately, and are claiming Moya as the property of the Consortium of Liantac.*"

"You've *got* to be kidding me."

Aeryn shook her head. *I knew we shouldn't have come to this place.* "Pilot, is the ship armed?"

"*No.*"

"Good. Put them through."

The face of a Lian male with bright red feathers appeared on the screen. "*Attention Leviathan crew. I am Wate, speaking on behalf of the Consortium of Liantac. Your ship is now the property of Netoros of the Consortium. Please proceed to one of your transport pods and disembark on the surface of Liantac. An officer of the Consortium will meet you and take the pod back to the Leviathan. Please accede to this request immediately.*"

"I'm Commander John Crichton, speaking on behalf of Moya's crew. We don't recognize the authority of the Consortium to claim our ship."

"*I'm afraid you must. The deed to the ship was turned over to Netoros in a proper gambling transaction by Dominar Rygel XVI. I repeat, disembark immediately.*"

Aeryn closed her eyes and took a deep breath.

Crichton muttered, "Oh, Sparky, what've you done *this* time?" Then, in a louder voice, he continued, "Dominar Rygel doesn't have the authority to use Moya in any transaction, nor does he possess any 'deed' to her, so there ain't nothin' 'proper' 'bout it, Wate. Kindly pack up your toys and go home, 'cause you ain't gettin' our ship."

"*You're in Liantac orbit, Commander. Until this matter is settled, the Clorium field will remain and prevent your Leviathan from leaving. As long as you remain in orbit, you are bound by our laws. According to those laws, Dominar Rygel XVI included your ship as part of a bet in a*" game of Haunan. He lost that game, and therefore lost the ship. It belongs to Netoros, and she is claiming it."

"Go to hell."

Wate stared at the screen for several microts. Then, finally, he spoke. *"I will convey your response to Netoros. We will talk again within the arn."*

The screen winked off.

Aeryn turned to Crichton. "The next time I say that going to a planet is a bad idea, I really hope you all have the brains to *listen* to me."

"And I was just gonna say there was no need to say 'I told you so'," Crichton muttered.

CHAPTER 4

W*ell, now this is a major letdown*, Crichton thought as he maneuvered the transport pod toward the Casino's hangar bay. Aeryn had warned Crichton that the lights would be blinding, but, so far, this place had nothing on Vegas.

Crichton had left Aeryn behind to keep Moya and Pilot—not to mention Wate and his ships—company while he went down to meet with Netoros to work out the "problem" that had resulted from Rygel's wager. Now he was getting his first glimpse of the Casino, which looked surprisingly dull to his eyes.

That's it entirely, he realized after thinking about it for a moment. Most of the races in this part of the galaxy, including all those on Moya, had significantly more acute eyesight than humans, so their garishness threshold was a good deal lower than his.

Aeryn had also warned him about the perky hologram that would torture him on the way down, and that warning, at least, had proven beneficial. Crichton hadn't seen such aggressive happiness since the last time he went to Disneyland. He acknowledged the instructions as to which hangar bay to go to, but otherwise ignored the hologram as best he could. After paying the retri for the first four arns, he proceeded on foot to the complex within the Casino that housed Netoros's office.

"Vi-i-i-i-va Las Vegas," he muttered. *Some of the colors are different, and the tech is a lot higher, but damn if this ain't just a poor imitation of Vegas. Same ostentation, same tackiness, same worship of cold, hard cash.*

And the same noise level. His ears were assaulted by a cacophony of sounds, ranging from the endless advertisements, to the music coming through the open doors of the various entertainment establishments all competing for clientele, to just the noise made by the throngs of life forms simply out to have a good time. *Even the commerce planets we've been to haven't been this hard on the ears*, he mused.

By the time he reached the office complex, Crichton had seen over a dozen advertisements, been solicited five times, and had a dozen chips pressed into his hand.

Rygel was waiting for him outside the complex, which adjoined Netoros's gaming establishment. Crichton assumed that Zhaan and D'Argo would be along soon. (They had called Chiana, but she hadn't answered her comm, though that didn't really surprise or worry any of them.) The Hynerian was wearing a black collar with a stylized, glowing red logo.

"Love the jewelery," Crichton quipped as he pocketed the chips.

"Oh, very amusing," Rygel said dolefully. "It isn't jewelery, you yotz, it's a restriction collar. It keeps the wearer from moving outside any of the designated areas—all of the Casino, and the residences in the city immediately surrounding."

"That's it?"

"That's it. The hangar bay, just in case you were wondering, is *not* a designated area, and neither is any place offplanet."

"I reckon I coulda sussed that one out on my own, Sparky," Crichton said with an exaggerated drawl. "What happens if you cross the line?"

"It imparts an electrical charge—rather a nasty one at that."

"Already tested it, huh?"

"Of course," Rygel said, as if it were the most natural thing in the world. "The first thing you learn when you're a prisoner, Crichton, is that you never take the jailer's word for it that the lock works."

The collar reminded Crichton of the control collar that they'd had to remove from Moya in order to escape the Peacekeepers. Or the one Chiana had been wearing when that creep Salis had brought her on board Moya as a prisoner. *Or*, he thought, *the ankle bracelets they put on people under house arrest back home*.

"What's most maddening," Rygel continued, "is that I was cheated!"

"Sure you were," Crichton said, rolling his eyes.

"I *was*! I wouldn't expect someone like you to under-stand, Crichton, but I've been gambling since before your ancestors were born, and I can assure you that I know when I've been cheated. Do you honestly think I would have bet Moya if there was even the slightest possibility that I would lose?"

"Rygel, even I know that the first rule of places like this is that the house always wins."

Amazingly enough, Rygel didn't have anything to say to that.

D'Argo soon arrived—giving Rygel his nastiest you-will-die-slowly-and-in-writhing-agony look—followed by Zhaan. D'Argo did not have his Qualta Blade, and Crichton suspected that he had been forced to leave it behind some-where. *Folks at the Casino probably prefer it if you check your deadly weapons at the door. That probably isn't im-proving the big guy's mood*, he reflected.

The four of them entered the complex, and took an ele-vator that deposited Crichton on the top floor about eighty microts before it got around to bringing his stomach up. There they were met by a short Lian woman sitting behind a desk. "We're here to see Netoros," Crichton told her.

"Ah yes. Just one moment." She pressed a button. "Netoros, Dominar Rygel and his party are here."

"Thank you, Celong, send them in."

Though D'Argo gave the Hynerian an angry look, Rygel couldn't suppress a smug smile at hearing the others called "his party."

Celong led them through a large door that was emblazoned with the same logo that was on Rygel's collar.

The office was one of the biggest Crichton had ever seen. *The only time I ever saw an office this enormous was when Dad got DK and me a tour of some bigwig's office up on Capitol Hill.*

Netoros's workspace had a huge metallic monstrosity of a desk with a few carefully arranged items on it. *That desk belongs to someone who never works at it*, Crichton thought. The bigwig's desk back in Washington had been much the same—it had been his assistants' offices that had looked like they'd been hit by a tornado.

Surrounding the desk were soft-cushioned chairs that looked like beanbags, a metal cabinet full of food and drink, and several holographic projectors, many of which showed a variety of indoor vistas. Crichton assumed they were the security cameras for Netoros's properties in the Casino, especially as they all went opaque as soon as Crichton and the others walked in.

"Thank you all for coming," Netoros said from behind the desk. "Please, have a seat."

Crichton sat in one of the beanbag-like chairs. As soon as his body touched the surface, the seat seemed to undulate. Crichton shot back up. "Whoa! That thing's alive."

D'Argo simply let out a low growl. Zhaan, whose seat was also moving, said calmly, "John, these are conformer chairs. They adjust themselves to provide maximum comfort once you sit in them."

"Oh," Crichton said lamely. *Once again, the human gets to be the dumb hick cousin that don't understand the ways of them thar big city folk.* "Sorry, they, ah, they don't have these where I come from." He sat back down again, this time more gingerly. The movements of the chair felt vaguely erotic, and Crichton wasn't sure he liked it.

"Yes, and from what I understand, you come from quite a ways away," Netoros said enigmatically.

Red alert, Crichton thought. "What's that supposed to mean?"

"All in good time, Commander Crichton."

Crichton didn't like the sound of that at all.

However, now that the chair had settled down, he rather liked the feel of it. In fact, he would venture to say that it was the most comfortable seat he'd ever been in in his life.

"Now then," Netoros said, looking at each of them in turn, "it seems we have a bit of a problem."

"No," D'Argo said, "you and Rygel have 'a bit of a problem'. How you work it out is your concern. My— our—concern," he amended with a brief, contrite look at Crichton and Zhaan, "is that you free Moya immediately."

"I'm afraid that's impossible. By the laws of Liantac, the Leviathan belongs to me, as per the rules of the Haunan game. And I control the Clorium field that's keeping the ship here."

"Possession is nine-tenths of the law, huh?" Crichton said with a snort.

Netoros gazed upon him. "An interesting aphorism. I would argue that it is ten-tenths."

"I don't care how many tenths it is," D'Argo shot back, "nor do I care about *any* of the laws of Liantac!"

"You should. You are in orbit of Liantac. Besides which, even if you ignore the fact that the Leviathan is part of the dominar's debt, he still *does* owe me a debt. The same law that requires him to wear that collar also requires that the debtor's ship not be able to depart from Liantac until the debt is paid. Admittedly, that law hasn't been enacted in thirty cycles, but it is still law. Until we find a way to settle this, the Clorium field will remain."

At that point, something occurred to Crichton. "Won't the field keep your techno-organic ferries away from the planet, too? That's your only way to get folks from off-world. Sounds to me like you're cutting off your—uh—beak to spite your face."

"Clorium only adversely affects Leviathans. Our ferries are not affected by the element at all."

Ah, well, Crichton thought with a sigh, *I tried.*

"In any case," Netoros went on, "we have three options. The first is the most obvious: you relinquish control of the Leviathan, thus fulfilling Dominar Rygel's debt to me . . ."

"That is *not* acceptable," D'Argo interrupted.

"D'Argo, please, let her finish," Zhaan said, her gentle tones in marked contrast to D'Argo's bluster.

The Luxan growled.

As if D'Argo hadn't spoken, Netoros continued. "The second option is to alert the Peacekeepers to your presence here. I happen to know that there is still a considerable bounty being offered for the capture of three of you, and I also happen to know that there's a high-ranking Peacekeeper scientist named Scorpius who has an interest in Commander Crichton here."

Blinking, Crichton asked, "How do you *know* all this?"

Netoros laughed. "Please, Commander. I run a gambling establishment and several taverns. The only people who talk more than drunks are gamblers, and we are quite well stocked with both. While officially the Peacekeepers have declared this planet to be off-limits and refuse to have anything to do with us, the fact of the matter is that plenty of them come here for relaxation or shore leave—as do others in a position to know about the inner workings of the Peacekeepers. One doesn't get to my position without paying attention to what's going on in the surrounding galaxy. Besides, I could hardly miss Captain Crais's beacon offering a reward for Ka D'Argo, Pa'u Zotoh Zhaan, and Dominar Rygel XVI."

"That's why you were so eager to get me into your Haunan game," Rygel said.

"Well, how often does one get the opportunity to play Haunan with a famous fugitive?"

"Okay, fine," Crichton said, "so you've got your ear to the ground, your nose to the grindstone, and your bats in the belfry. I think you know that we don't like either of those two options. What's behind door number three, Monty?"

Netoros stared at Crichton for a moment, then said, "The third option is one that I think we will all find beneficial. Frankly, I'd rather not antagonize someone who has managed to evade Peacekeeper capture for two cycles, and I know you'd rather not give up your ship. Therefore the third option is to find an alternative way for you to work off Rygel's wager."

"Unacceptable," D'Argo said flatly.

"D'Argo, will you at least let her finish?" Crichton said.

"Fine," D'Argo said. "Make your offer so we can refuse it and leave."

Netoros got up and walked slowly around the desk. "My offer is simple. There are three services I require that three of you are ideally suited for. Perhaps you have seen advertisements for a singer named Licit at the Harilear Club?"

"I have," Zhaan said. "In fact, I was offered free passes earlier today."

Working her way slowly behind each of the four Moya crew, Netoros continued, "I own the Harilear Club, and Licit is my biggest draw. Unfortunately, as will sometimes happen, he has had death threats made against him. In this case, it is a gentleman who insists that his beloved has left him because she's hopelessly in love with Licit. Personally, I doubt the threats are serious, but Licit says he won't perform unless I provide him with some protection. I suspect that this particular person's obsession is playing to Licit's ego so much that he feels the need to take it seriously." Netoros was now behind D'Argo, and she put a hand on his shoulder. "In any event, a fierce Luxan warrior would make a fine bodyguard. It would only be for a few solar days until I can calm him down and convince him that there's no threat—besides, if it looks like I imported a bodyguard from offworld, it will placate him. Artists are notoriously mercurial, so I'm sure this will pass."

"Quiet, D'Argo," Crichton said as the Luxan opened his mouth, presumably to start another tirade. The words earned Crichton a fierce glower. Pointedly ignoring it, Crichton prompted, "What else?"

Removing her hand from D'Argo's shoulder, Netoros moved to Zhaan. "I understand, Zhaan, that you are well versed in the ways of exotic plants?"

"I have some expertise," Zhaan replied neutrally.

"For reasons that should be fairly obvious, that is not a skill that many here have. A fellow member of the Consortium, Garess, is something of a collector. He has recently acquired several new offworld plants that he cannot identify. I would like you to catalogue them for him."

"What's in that for you?"

"Don't be an idiot, Crichton," Rygel said testily. "If this Garess is a member of the Consortium, and Zhaan does a favor for him on Netoros's behalf, Garess is in her debt."

"Exactly," Netoros said. Turning to Crichton, "As for 'door number three', as you put it, that would be you, Commander. A little under a cycle ago, an officer who had been assigned to Scorpius came here. He was quite taciturn— until he started losing. And drinking. A talkative drunk, he had all sorts of things to say about a being who looked Sebacean but wasn't, and who knew a surprising amount about propulsion systems, including some kind of slingshot maneuver—and about wormholes."

Crichton started. "I don't—"

Netoros held up a hand. "Please, Commander, I don't wish to subject you to torture or learn what deep, dark secrets about wormholes you might have. Personally, I've always thought wormholes to be a myth. But you *do* know about propulsion, and you did build your own spacecraft, yes?"

"Yeah." Crichton shifted uncomfortably in his comfortable seat. *This woman knows way too much*, he thought.

"Then perhaps you can succeed where others have failed. For thirty cycles, we have tried to figure out a way to get ships to function amidst the larik particles that choke Liantac's bonosphere. Nothing has worked."

"Yeah, but you've got the ferries," Crichton said.

"Barely. The techno-organic technology still hasn't been perfected. They're inefficient, they use obscene amounts of fuel, and they break down very quickly." She chuckled. "Actually, they don't so much break down as rot. We're still not sure why they rot, but once that happens, they can't be fixed, and they're prohibitively expensive to replace. It's curtailed offworld traffic to a degree that may soon destroy our economy."

Crichton looked at Netoros as if she were crazy, a diagnosis he was beginning to warm to—though he had to admit to being a bit flattered at her comments about his technical know-how. "And you expect *me* to be able to solve this problem?"

"Honestly? No. But I also have nothing to lose by asking you to try and quite a bit to gain if you do somehow succeed. All I ask of you is that you examine the problem for the time it will take D'Argo to assuage Licit and Zhaan to identify Garess's flora."

Crichton leaned back. He had the fight the urge to nod off, the seat was so comfortable . . .

That, in turn, made him more alert. Putting her guests at ease like this was probably why Netoros had such comfortable seats in the first place. Crichton wasn't about to let himself be so easily manipulated.

"So let's say we do this," he said. "Then we're free to go?"

"Of course," Netoros said. "The debt will be fulfilled."

D'Argo stood up with surprising speed. "As I said before, the debt is between you and Rygel. I will not participate in this foolishness."

With that, he stormed out of the office.

Crichton struggled to get out of his seat. "I'll talk to him."

Netoros said, "So you will do it?"

"I don't see why not."

"D'Argo does."

Moving toward the door, Crichton said, "Like I said, I'll talk to him. Trust me. We'll be back before you know it."

"I hope so, Commander. Because if you do not agree to all three terms, we will have to go back to the second plan—the one where I turn you in to the Peacekeepers."

Nodding grimly, Crichton left Netoros's office.

One belly-bombing ride down the lift later, he found D'Argo on a passageway outside the door to the complex. The Luxan stood with his arms folded, staring straight ahead.

Without even looking at him, D'Argo said, "I know what you're going to say, Crichton. The answer is no."

"Look, will you just think about it for a second? We're stuck here until Sparky settles the debt no matter what. Why not take the easy way out and do what she asks?"

"I see no reason to humor some imbecile singer because of that Hynerian fool."

"C'mon, D'Argo, all you have to do is stand around and growl a lot. You do that anyhow."

D'Argo made a noise in the back of his throat.

"Just play Costner to this guy's Whitney for a few days, and then we're outta here. How bad can it be?"

"Do you really want me to answer that?"

Crichton had to concede that point. "All right, fine, but think about this: what if he really is in danger? You could be saving the guy's life."

"Netoros said the threat was imaginary."

"If it is, then the job's real easy. If it isn't, you get a chance to save someone's life in battle. Tell me you don't like that idea."

"I don't like that idea."

"Well, I don't like the idea of being turned over to

58   Keith R. A. DeCandido

Scorpy and you guys going back into the clink, but that's
what's gonna happen if you don't do this."

Making a derisive noise, D'Argo said, "She is bluffing.
This planet isn't even accessible to offworlders."

"Look around, D'Argo," Crichton began, pointing at the
pedestrians who milled about, only about half of whom
were Lians. "This place is crawling with Sebaceans, Nebari,
Luxans, Tavleks—hell, I saw a Scarren on my way here.
And Netoros knows about that wanted beacon that Aeryn
and I saw at the Dam-Ba-Da Depot last year, and she knows
way too much about Scorpy's designs on my brain. If she
is bluffing, it's good enough that I'd rather fold than call."

D'Argo stared at Crichton for several microts. It had
taken a long time for him to learn to read the Luxan's
expressions—there was so much, well, *stuff* on his face that
it could be difficult to tell what he was thinking through all
the tentacles, braids, tattoos, and facial hair. *Now, though,
I'm pretty sure the big lug's gonna give in*.

Finally, D'Argo said, "Will you and Zhaan do as Netoros
asks?"

"Yeah. Zhaan will probably enjoy it—and to be honest,
so will I. It'll be nice to sink my teeth into a good old-
fashioned techie problem for a change."

D'Argo sighed. "Very well. I will do this—but only for
three solar days. No more."

"That's fine."

"Good."

Crichton headed back inside. "Now can we please go tell
her that and get on with it?"

D'Argo said nothing, but merely walked back to the entrance.

As soon as D'Argo turned away from him, Crichton let
out a long breath. *First landmine dodged. Can't wait to see
how Aeryn reacts*.

"You're out of your minds, you know that."

"Thank you so much for that newsflash, Aeryn, but we

don't have much choice. If we don't, she sics Scorpy and the Peacekeepers on us."

It had been a quarter arn since the meeting with Netoros ended, and Crichton had been getting grief from Aeryn the whole time. Even over the comm, he could hear the irritation in her voice. Leaning against the wall outside the hangar bay, he watched Rygel float around. The dominar's collar prevented him from entering the hangar bay, which forced them to wait for the others outside. Zhaan had gone off to fetch Chiana, while D'Argo went to retrieve his Qualta. Crichton had contacted Aeryn in the hope of getting her input on the game plan. So far, her only input had been to question his sanity.

"I told you we shouldn't have come to this frelling planet. I—"

"Give it a rest, Aeryn."

"If she's going on about something," said a deep voice from behind Crichton, "she's probably right."

Crichton turned to see D'Argo returning with his Qualta Blade secure on his back. As Crichton had suspected, he had had to check the blade at the hangar upon his arrival, as no one was permitted weapons inside the Casino apart from authorized personnel. Netoros had just provided D'Argo with a small badge that identified him as a security employee of hers, thus authorizing him to carry his weapon.

Crichton grinned. "Congrats, D'Argo, you look like you again."

"What are you talking about? I always look like me. Except when I was in Pilot's and Chiana's bodies, of course . . ."

"It's the blade. Puts that nice homicidal glint back in your eye."

Rygel muttered, "He always has a homicidal glint in his eye."

Before D'Argo could reply, Zhaan and Chiana both approached. Looking straight at Rygel, Chiana asked, "How could you lose Moya in a *Haunan game*?"

"Can we *please* put a lid on the recriminations?" Crichton said with a sigh. "Fact: Rygel's a schmuck. Let's move on, okay?"

"I'm telling you, I was *cheated*," Rygel said, tugging angrily at his collar. "And," he added, "this frelling collar itches."

"Now you know how I felt," Chiana muttered. "Anyway, I've got some news."

She proceeded to explain her suspicions about Rari.

"You're basing this on a hesitation?" Aeryn said, sounding dubious.

"It's more than that. Look, I know from liars, all right? And this guy was lying."

"We'll certainly bow to your superior knowledge on that subject," Aeryn said drily.

"If Pip's right, this is starting to get ugly," Crichton mused. "First Rari deliberately gets us here, then Netoros makes sure Rygel's invited to her personal Haunan game."

"Not just that," Rygel said. "I was approached by several people who enticed me to the House of Games in the first place."

D'Argo said, "She could not *possibly* have planned Rygel losing Moya."

"I'm telling you, she *did* plan it!" Rygel said angrily. "She cheated me!"

"Look, it doesn't matter," Crichton said. "Let's just do what she wants us to do. With any luck, that'll be that, and we can get outta here."

"What if that isn't that?"

"What do you mean, Aeryn?" Zhaan asked.

"I mean, what if Netoros decides that this won't be sufficient to pay the debt? Or what if this is just a delaying tactic so she can get the Peacekeepers here?"

"The bounty for our capture is considerable," Zhaan said, "but it's a pittance to someone like Netoros. Even if you consider how economically damaged Liantac has become, she is still one of the wealthiest people on the planet. Simply turning us in to the Peacekeepers would not be sufficient reason for her to delay us."

"Besides, she already has us trapped here," Chiana said.

"Yes, but this way she can keep an eye on us," Rygel pointed out. "Aeryn could be correct."

"Rygel and I agree?" Aeryn said. *"Things are worse than I thought."*

"Either way," Crichton said, "I think we should play along. All right, maybe she is playing us for saps and won't forgive the debt if we do all this—but I can tell you one thing, she *definitely* won't forgive the debt if we *don't* do it."

"John is correct," Zhaan said. "Even if Netoros does not fulfill her end of the bargain, I believe that we should fulfill ours."

"Her bargain with *Rygel*, you mean," D'Argo muttered.

"We can do a little more than that," Crichton said. "Chiana, we're gonna need you to finish Zhaan and D'Argo's shopping trip."

"Fine," Chiana said with a smile.

Crichton knew that smile all too well. "You're *buying*, not stealing, 'kay, Pip?"

"You never let me have *any* fun," Chiana said, visibly deflating.

"Yeah, and don't you forget it."

"Frelling wonderful," Aeryn said.

"There a problem, Aeryn?" Crichton asked.

"No more than usual. Chiana, read the list carefully, all right? Any parts that don't match what we ask for, you eat."

"Why doesn't anybody trust me?" Chiana asked with a small pout.

"Well, let's see—there was the time you brought the Vorc on board and it peed all over D'Argo and tried to frell my leg. There was that lovely portrait from Maldis that nearly got us all killed. Then—"

"Point taken, Aeryn," Crichton said, "but we don't have much choice. Zhaan, D'Argo and I'll be busy, and the alternative is to let Rygel do the shopping."

"You must be joking," Rygel said. "I do not 'shop'."

"That does raise an important question," Zhaan said. "What do we do with Rygel?"

"I beg your pardon," Rygel said, his ears rising. "You don't 'do' anything with me! I'm perfectly capable of looking after myself, thank you."

"Sparky, the last time you looked after yourself, you lost the ship," Crichton said.

"I will take Rygel," said Zhaan. "He is unlikely to get into any more trouble with me."

"I protest this," Rygel said. "I am Dominar Ry—"

With astonishing speed, D'Argo reached out and grabbed Rygel by what passed for his neck. 'You will either go with Zhaan or you will go with me. Choose."

Rygel sputtered a few times, then said, "Zh-Zhaan."

D'Argo let go. "Wise choice."

"And let's keep our ears to the ground, okay?" Crichton added. "Talk to people. Find out what they think."

"About what?" D'Argo asked.

"Netoros. The Consortium. Gambling. The larik particles. The singing, the dancing, the price of tea in China, whatever. If Netoros does pull a double-cross, we'll be better off if we know the playing field."

I've gotta stop mixing my metaphors, Crichton thought with a small grin. *Like anybody here'd notice.*

"Let's go and get this over with, then," D'Argo said.

"I made some friends when I went bar-hopping with Rari," Chiana said, wearing that smile of hers again. "Maybe some of them will open up."

Remembering Netoros's comment about chatty drunks and gamblers, Crichton agreed. "Sounds good. And Aeryn? Keep us posted on Wate."

"Actually, Wate just moved off".

Snorting, Crichton said, "Maybe his ship's starting to rot."

"Either way, the Clorium field's still in place, which is the only thing that matters."

"Yeah." Crichton smiled. "All right, people, we've got our mission, should we choose to accept it. Remember, if we're caught, the secretary will disavow any knowledge of our actions."

Both Rygel and D'Argo made the same grunt in response to that. Zhaan, though, smiled as she led Rygel off.

CHAPTER 5

Licit finished his last song of the evening—his fourth encore, a reprise of his most popular love song, "The Sun Never Rises." Licit frankly hated the tune, but the people would riot if he didn't do it at least once, and most insisted that he reprise it at the end. He generally saved it for his absolutely last encore, since he often had the urge to be sick after singing it twice in one set. To make matters worse, he'd have to sing it twice more at the second show later that night.

As the stage went dark and the holographic scrim went up across the stagefront, Licit headed backstage, trying to get to his dressing room as fast as he could. *You never know whether or not he's out there*, he thought, referring to the little eema that had threatened his life. *And he is. I know he is. He was probably in the audience, watching me the whole time.*

Licit wasn't sure he could handle this pressure anymore. *If only Netoros would take me seriously!*

But she wouldn't. All she cared about was the money

Licit brought in. "It's all in your head," she'd insist. "It's just the usual cranks," she'd scoff. And Reis, his manager, was just as bad—but then, the only opinions Reis ever had were the ones Netoros gave him.

As he approached his dressing room, he saw Netoros, Reis, and an enormous Luxan standing by the door.

"Great show, Licit, great show," Reis said unctuously.

Licit ignored him, as usual. "Who's this?"

"This is Ka D'Argo," Netoros said. "D'Argo, this is Licit, your new assignment."

"Assignment?" Licit asked.

"D'Argo is a Luxan," his manager added.

"Oh, thanks *so* much, Reis. And here I thought he was a Halosian. Silly me." Turning back to Netoros, he asked, "What is this individual's purpose?"

"He is to be your bodyguard. I want you to see, Licit, that I *do* take your concerns seriously. I brought D'Argo here from offworld just to protect you. D'Argo is to accompany you everywhere until this person who has threatened your life is taken care of."

Licit was impressed, though he would never have admitted it to Netoros.

"He'll do, I suppose," he said casually, while moving toward his dressing room.

D'Argo grabbed Licit's arm with one meaty hand, holding him firmly in place. "What're you doing? Take your hands off me! How *dare* you touch me!" Licit shouted.

His hand remaining where it was, the Luxan asked, "Has anyone been in this dressing room since you were in it last?"

"How should I know?"

D'Argo unsheathed his sword. "Wait here," he said.

"I will not stand outside my—"

"Wait here," the Luxan repeated, "until I can secure the dressing room."

That brought Licit up short. "Secure?"

"That's what bodyguards *do*, Licit," Netoros said. "So let him do his work."

Licit sighed. "Very well."

The Luxan waved his hand over the door sensor, and it opened. He went in slowly. *Why's the imbecile holding his sword like it was a gun?* thought Licit. *What kind of frelling idiot did Netoros hire for me?*

"The room is secure," the Luxan said after a few microts.

Licit was less impressed than he had been a few microts ago.

Still, he thought with a sigh, *I suppose it'll have to do. It's not like Netoros will do any better for me.*

"Thank you, Netoros, Reis. If you'll excuse me, I'm tired and I want to change and get in a quick nap and a meal before the second show. Not to mention my drink."

Frowning, Netoros said, "Licit, if you're so afraid of this person, why expose yourself by going out into the bar?"

Licit looked at Netoros in disbelief, mixed with more than a little disgust. "Because my fans expect it." *Thori's beak, but that woman can be obtuse,* he thought. *How did someone so ignorant of the realities of the entertainment business come to run a house of entertainment?*

"Don't forget," Reis said, "you also have the recording session with Rosin Hous tomorrow."

Licit blinked. "Who?"

"The Sebacean singer."

"Fine, whatever." Licit couldn't keep track of all the commitments he made. That was why he kept Reis around. *It certainly isn't for his sterling personality,* he reflected. "Just send Taris, as usual."

"Who is Taris?" the Luxan asked.

"She's Licit's chauffeur," Reis said. "She's driven Licit everywhere since he first started performing at the Harilear."

"She's safe," Netoros said.

"Of course she's safe, she's my cousin," Reis said in a tone that was no doubt meant to convey an indignant tone, but always sounded to Licit like a whine.

"Very well," the Luxan said, nodding.

Shooing Reis and Netoros out the door, Licit said, "Goodbye, both of you." The door closed on them.

Licit started to remove his clothing. *I can't get out of this frelling tunic fast enough.* Everybody always said he looked incredibly attractive in it—and the women certainly loved it—but it was heavy, and he was always happy to be rid of it.

As he undressed, Licit addressed D'Argo brusquely. "All right, Luxan, here's the deal. You are to be by my side at all times, except when I'm taking care of private bodily functions. No one is to come anywhere near me without going through you first. The obvious exception is Netoros."

"And Reis, I assume."

"No, he doesn't need to get near me. In fact, I'm generally happier when he isn't. I want my food tested, every room I go into checked. I want—"

"I know how to protect someone."

How dare he interrupt! "You work for *me*, Luxan, do you understand that?"

"No, I don't. I work for Netoros."

"You impertinent grolash! Another rule, Luxan, is that you speak when spoken to, is that clear?"

The Luxan walked over to Licit, who by now was down to his underwear, and suddenly very conscious of the fact. The alien loomed over him, still holding that sword of his. "I want you to understand something, Licit. I am here to protect you. How I do that is my concern, not yours. I will do this my way or no way at all. Is *that* clear?"

Licit swallowed. "I—I'm going to speak to Netoros about you. What—whatever she's paying you is too much, and—and I'll see to it that you're fired!"

"To be honest, Licit, I'm not getting paid nearly enough. Now hurry up and get dressed. The sight of you is making me ill."

"The sight of you has been making me ill since I first saw you, Luxan," Licit muttered as he put a fresh shirt on. "What are those obscene tattoos on your chin and head, anyhow?"

"A chronicle of all the people I've killed because they annoyed me."

Licit swallowed again.

First thing tomorrow, I'm calling Netoros and getting a replacement. Imagine, killing people because they annoyed him!

Unless—he was joking. Yes, that's it. Joking.

So why isn't he smiling?

Licit got dressed faster.

Chiana had had no idea there were so many herbs and potions in the galaxy, although by now she was pretty sure she'd got the ones Zhaan wanted. *Well, too bad if I didn't. I'm not a frelling healer.*

She really didn't want to deal with Aeryn and Crichton's shopping list until she'd had a drink. So she stopped at the hangar bay, locked Zhaan's goodies in the transport pod, and then headed out in search of an appropriate watering hole.

Not surprisingly, she found herself back at Terisears's. It was, after all, the only place she and Rari had gone that she had actually liked.

Terisears was still tending bar. "Well, well, well," she said, "you're back. And without Rari this time."

"He couldn't keep up with me. I'll have another one of those sunsets."

"Coming right up," Terisears said.

As she prepared the drink, an older Lian sat down next to her. At least, Chiana assumed he was older, since his face was wrinkled, his feathers were as white as Chiana's own hair, and his beak looked gnarled.

"Now this is a sight for old eyes," he said. "I'm Yalla."

"Chiana." She reached forward and squeezed the old man's shoulder.

That made Yalla straighten right up. He returned the gesture with a grip that was a bit arthritic, but firm nonetheless.

"What brings your pretty face to this dreary bar?" he asked.

Just as Terisears placed a bowl in front of Chiana, she

purred, "I came for the sunsets, of course. Doesn't every-body?" She leaned forward and slowly lapped up a bit. *Oh, after dealing with those stupid plants, I needed that*, she thought as the tingling sensation hit.

"Everybody sensible does, yes," Yalla said with a laugh. "Speaking of which, one for me, Terisears. Anyhow, that usually leaves out offworlders. How'd you even find out about this place?"

"Rari brought her here," Terisears said as she prepared a second sunset.

Yalla blinked. "Rari? He's finally back? About frelling time the little zark got his beak back here."

Smiling, Chiana queried, "He owe you money?"

"How'd you know?"

"Instinct. People who leave home for cycles at a time usually owe money."

"And how would you know that?" Yalla asked as Teri-sears placed the sunset in front of him.

"Why do you think I left *my* homeworld?" she said with a wide grin.

Yalla laughed. "I'll have to be sure not to lend you money, then."

"Probably wise. Anyway, I'm sure Rari'll be able to pay you back. He certainly paid us enough to bring him here."

"I guess he found his valuable person, then."

Chiana frowned. "Valuable person?"

"Something like that. When he left, he said he was going to hook up with a trading ship of some kind. Had to go find 'a valuable person'. Or maybe it was 'valuable people', I forget which. Believe it or not, I'm getting old and my memory's starting to go."

"You're not old," Chiana said, remembering that, ac-cording to Rygel, Lians were somewhat short-lived, much like Crichton's people. "C'mon, you can't be more than forty cycles old."

Again Yalla laughed. "My dear, you are either unflag-gingly polite or extremely blind. I'm going to celebrate my sixtieth cycle tomorrow."

"Well, happy birthday, then, Yalla," she said with another squeeze of his shoulder.

"Thank you, Chiana."

They each lapped up some of their sunsets.

"Out of curiosity," she asked, leaning closer to Yalla and speaking in a very low, almost conspiratorial, whisper, "do you know what kind of trading ship he was going on?"

It didn't take Crichton long to get used to the computer terminal. True, he hadn't operated anything like it before, but he'd become accustomed to Moya's systems fairly quickly. While the Liantac computers were, naturally, different from those on a Leviathan, the differences were no greater than those between the Apple computers he'd used in college and the mainframe he'd used in graduate school. *Like going from LINUX to UNIX—or a Mac to a PC, for that matter*, he thought.

Unlike the others, he had gone back to the office complex where they met Netoros. Her assistant—the no-nonsense woman named Celong—had taken him to a small, undecorated office. The room was equipped with a desk, a computer terminal, and a chair. It didn't even have a window, but given that the best he could've gotten was a view of the Casino's lights, Crichton figured that, at least, was for the best.

Crichton rearranged the control pad so that it was comfortable for him—his ergonomic requirements were somewhat different from those of the longer-armed Lians—then started going through the computer's available directories. It had been programmed with all the information Liantac's scientists had collected about the larik particles, as well as the details as to how they'd come to poison the bonosphere.

Unsurprisingly, the catastrophe had come about because of gambling—specifically, two people who had played each other in Tadek. The loser—who owned the largest ship-repair facility on Liantac—wanted revenge on the winner, so he sabotaged the winner's ship with larik particles. The intent was to stall the ship out, ruin the engine, and force the winner to pay an exorbitant repair fee to the loser to fix it. *Almost sounds like something Rygel would do*, Crichton mused.

Unfortunately, larik particles were organic, and reproduced at a great rate when taken out of stasis. As a result, the minute amount of particles that the loser started with continued to replicate and, rather than simply stall the engine, blew up the ship. Worse, the ship had been in the bonosphere, right in the jet stream—within seventy-five arns, the particles had completely encircled Liantac.

Like the locusts in Egypt. And they call me an ignorant savage. From the moment the wormhole had dumped Crichton on this side of the galaxy, he'd had a significant amount of chauvinism shoved in his face, just because his race was so technologically backward as to be unable to leave their own star system. *But if I've learned nothing else the last couple of cycles, it's that life forms are stupid everywhere, whether they can go faster than light or not.*

Every attempt to get rid of the larik particles had failed. The best the Lians could do was to find a way around it rather than a way to fix it, so that commerce could continue.

After going through the background, Crichton studied the larik particles themselves. *Interesting chemical composition*, he thought as he examined the data. It confirmed what Pilot had told him: the antibodies in a biological ship like Moya or the ferries would treat the larik particles like a virus and expel them.

There's got to be some way to adapt that for an inorganic ship, he thought.

Crichton had no idea if he could find it, but he was thrilled at the chance to try. He'd had precious few opportunities to flex his scientific muscles since arriving on Moya, and when he did, it was usually in a crisis situation. *It'll be nice to play Brainiac without the seat of my pants getting involved.*

As he started to turn his mind to it, Rygel's voice sounded from his comm. *"Crichton, are you there?"*

"I'm a little busy, Sparky, what's up?" Crichton asked.

"My boredom level. I'm trapped in this yotz Garess's house while Zhaan communes with her fellow plants and Garess talks on his comm all the time making deals."

"So relax, Rygel. Take a nap. Read a book. Pick your toenails. I don't care. Better yet, eat something. That's your usual leisure activity, isn't it?"

"I have been eating. At least the kitchen is well stocked."

"Great. Jim-dandy. If you're bored, go eat some more. Maybe there's a crumb you missed somewhere. Now I've got work to do, so—"

"I don't. Besides, I had a thought."

"Must be lonely in there," Crichton muttered.

"I heard that."

"That was the idea. Get on with it."

"We can solve this entire problem if I go back to the Casino and win back my losses. Then I can pay Netoros legitimately and we can get the frell off this planet."

"Oh, good idea, Sparky. Then you can lose my module and Aeryn's Prowler at Tadek while you're at it—maybe get the rest of us sold into slavery over a friendly game of Go Fish. Why didn't *I* think of that?"

"Go Fish?"

"If we get through this, I'll teach it to you. For now, hang out with Zhaan. Or hell, hang out with Garess. Use that Hynerian charm on him, find out if he can give us any dirt on Netoros."

"Hmm. Perhaps you're right."

"Glory hallelujah, the little guy actually admits I'm right. I can die a happy man now."

"Your sarcasm is not appreciated, Crichton. We wouldn't be in this mess if you hadn't insisted on coming here."

Crichton blinked. 'Me? You're the one who said this place was the greatest thing since sliced bread."

"Yes, but despite my hundreds of cycles of experience in the universe, despite my position as a royal personage, and despite the fact that you're a yotz from a backward planet in the nether regions, the others always listen to you and

never listen to me. Just remember that if we never see the inside of Moya again."

With that, Rygel signed off.

Crichton sighed. *One of these days, I'm going to understand that little guy.*

Humming the tune to "Viva Las Vegas," he went back to work.

D'Argo stood backstage and tried very hard to resist the urge to strangle someone.

He had to remember to retract his statement to Crichton. Back on Moya, when the human had been trying and failing to re-create the lyrics to that frelling song of his, D'Argo had called it the worst noise he could imagine hearing.

Obviously, I didn't give my imagination enough credit, he thought. As bad as Crichton's disjointed singing was, it was heavenly compared to the dren Licit was caterwauling on stage right now.

So far, D'Argo's job had been easy enough. Licit generally kept to himself, which made protecting him all the easier. However, after this show he would go out for a drink in the bar and "mingle." Considering how paranoid Licit had been about letting anyone near him, this seemed an odd thing to do, but Licit had explained that he did it after *every* show.

"I can't very well let my fans down," he had told D'Argo.

"They would probably survive."

"Survive, yes, but they would not enjoy. I wouldn't expect you to understand the demands of fame, Luxan," Licit had added with a sneer.

After finishing the latest in an interminable series of songs, Licit thanked the screaming audience and at last came offstage. D'Argo began moving towards the dressing room.

"Where are you going?" asked Licit.

"To your dressing room. And so are you."

"No I'm not, you grolash. I have to do at least three more encores."

"Encores?"

"Yes, it's traditional when you've given a good performance and the audience applauds so much that—"

"I *know* what an encore is," D'Argo said testily. *I just don't understand why you would earn one*, he thought.

"Then you should know that I always do three, ending with a reprise of—" he hesitated, sighed and then finished, "—'The Sun Never Rises.' Thori's beak, but I hate that song."

"How can it be an encore if you *always* do the same thing?"

Licit spoke slowly, as if D'Argo were an infant. "Because that's what my fans expect, and I do not want to disappoint them. Now, if you'll excuse me . . ." Licit turned and went back onstage.

D'Argo ground his teeth.

As promised, Licit did three encores, ending with another rendition of "The Sun Never Rises," which managed to sound even more painful the second time.

After bowing far more times than D'Argo thought necessary, Licit came offstage. "Now come, let us meet my adoring public—but from a distance. And we'll only stay for a quarter of an arn."

He has some *sense at least*, D'Argo thought. "Good."

They wended their way through the Harilear's backstage area to the bar. A female fan screamed, cried out, "It's Licit! It's Licit!" and ran toward them.

D'Argo intercepted her and pushed her away. She fell to the ground in a heap.

"He pushed me! He pushed me!" the fan cried in anguish as some people helped her up. D'Argo wondered if she was capable of doing anything but stating the blindingly obvious twice.

Others milled towards Licit but kept their distance. Several made comments such as, "Great show," or "I love your work," or "Thank you for playing 'Dayrider'." D'Argo glowered at anyone who got within arm's length. He'd come up with a rather ingenious way of keeping as unpleasant an expression on his face as possible: he imagined that everyone he saw was Rygel.

Licit was astonishingly polite as he navigated the sea of people to get to the bar, giving each person that came toward him a nod or wave. He even thanked some of them for their loyalty. D'Argo noticed that a drink was already waiting at the stool Licit chose for his seat. The Luxan reached towards the bowl, trying to decide who would test the liquid for poison. Before he could grab it, however, Licit bent over and lapped it up. "Ah, excellent. A fine vintage."

If he dies of poisoning, I will not *accept the blame*, D'Argo thought.

"Thanks, Licit," the bartender said with a nod. "Can I get you anything else?"

D'Argo tensed, hoping that Licit would decline.

Licit, naturally, took his time mulling it over.

Just as D'Argo was about to speak for the singer, Licit finally spoke up: "No, thank you." The Luxan breathed a sigh of relief.

The bartender leaned forward. In an almost conspiratorial whisper, she said, "You sure I can't tempt you with a plate of fried harrik? Cook says it's especially good tonight."

"It would be wise if you stuck with the drink," D'Argo said when it looked as though Licit might be wavering.

Ignoring the Luxan, Licit told the bartender, "It's a tempting thought, but no, not tonight. Perhaps tomorrow."

"Fair enough," the bartender replied. "Let me know if you need anything." She moved off to serve other customers.

A few more people called out congratulations to Licit, which he politely acknowledged. D'Argo guessed he could understand why Licit did this—it was a way of ingratiating himself with the people who supported him in his living—but it didn't make protecting him any easier.

Just three days, D'Argo thought. *I survived eight cycles in chains on Moya, I can survive three days of this hezmana.*

"Licit, my dear friend, how are you?" said a short Lian as he approached the bar. He had bright red feathers and a shirt with more colors than most of the signage in the Casino. His voice was as loud as his shirt. Given the ambient noise level, a normal voice wouldn't have been heard from as far away as he had started. As he moved closer, he bellowed, "It's *so* good to see you, as always."

"Uh, hello again, Tresser," Licit muttered. D'Argo could hear the dread in his voice.

"Great show once again, my good friend. Hey, I've got another recording for you to listen to if you want. I—"

Once he got within arm's reach, D'Argo's hand landed firmly on Tresser's chest. "That's close enough."

"Hey, Licit, call off your Luxan, huh? We're old buddies. Besides, I've got to give you this recording."

Not giving Licit a chance to answer, D'Argo said, "You will keep your distance."

"Look, I—"

"That was not a request, it was a statement of fact."

Tresser stood a head shorter than D'Argo, a fact the Luxan used to his advantage. He stood close enough to loom over Tresser, his hand was still firmly on the latter's chest.

"M-maybe I should—should just get—get going, huh? I mean, obviously Licit's a busy man, and—ah—"

"Good idea," D'Argo said, removing his hand.

"Can—can I at least give him the recor—"

"No."

"Okay. That's fine."

Tresser slunk off.

Licit looked up at D'Argo. "How did you do that?"

"Do what?"

"Get rid of Tresser."

D'Argo shrugged. "It was easy."

"You don't understand. Tresser has been the bane of my

existence for over a cycle. He's *constantly* hounding me with terrible recordings of him singing my songs. He thinks he's my best friend, and I can never get him to go away. Good work."

"Glad you're so delighted." D'Argo's voice dripped with sarcasm.

Licit waved. "Bartender!"

The woman walked over. "Yes, Licit?"

"A drink for my noble bodyguard, please."

"I do not require a drink," D'Argo said testily.

"Nonsense, I insist. A ker'it tonic, please—mustn't have anything alcoholic, of course, but all this work must build up a thirst."

The bartender nodded. "Coming right up."

"He's the one! He's the one!"

Not her again. D'Argo turned to see the fan he'd knocked over approaching, trailing one of the bouncers— a beefy Sebacean with a short haircut and no discernible neck.

"He knocked me over! He knocked me over! You should arrest him right now!" She pointed an accusing finger at D'Argo.

The Sebacean addressed D'Argo. "Sir, this female has made a rather serious accusation."

D'Argo turned to face the bouncer. "It's completely true. I was doing my job."

The bouncer's demeanor changed as soon as he saw the badge that D'Argo had affixed to his tunic. And it changed even more when he saw Licit. "You're Licit's new body-guard, yeah?"

"That is correct."

"Sorry to've bothered you then, sir." He bowed slightly and took the fan by the arm. "Come on, ma'am."

"Hey! Hey! You can't do this! He pushed me! He pushed me!" she wailed as the Sebacean took her away.

D'Argo sighed. *Just three frelling days.*

*   *   *

" 'Til we meet again," Chiana slurred as she stumbled slowly out of Terisears's, waving to Yalla.

Yalla, still sitting at the bar, waved back. "I will count the microts, my dear," he replied.

"And happy birthday!"

"If I spend it thinking of you, it will be a happy one indeed."

Chiana laughed drunkenly as the door to Terisears's closed behind her.

As soon as she rounded the corner, Chiana stopped stumbling and straightened up. *Well, that was educational*, she thought with perfect clarity.

From what Yalla had told her after three sunsets, Rari had hit a rough spot financially. Then, one day, a little over a cycle ago, he had gone off on a Luxan trader in search of those "important people."

Chiana was supposed to meet the others outside the hangar bay at midnight, after Licit's last show, and confer before she headed back to Moya with the fruits of the shopping trip. *Am I going to have something to tell them! Especially Aeryn. "You're basing this on a hesitation?" Damn right I was—and I was right. Put that in your pulse rifle and fire it . . .*

Chiana worked her way toward the monorail. She still had one more task to go: fetching engine parts for Aeryn and Crichton.

Unsurprisingly by now, the attendant who took her fare thanked her effusively for riding the monorail on the greatest planet in the galaxy.

While she was waiting on the platform, Chiana took several free passes to a variety of establishments that she had no intention of visiting. On the monorail—sponsored by some anonymous hotel—a man came in and preached the evils of gambling. The occupants of the rail displayed little interest in what he had to say, though Chiana suspected, based on the looks on many of the passengers' faces, they might have been better off if they'd taken the preacher's admonitions to heart. The nice thing about the preacher was that he drowned out the advertisement for Ornara's Emporium at the front of the car.

As Chiana maneuvered through the crowd on the platform after disembarking, a Lian male with speckled head feathers (some of which looked a bit bent) and wearing a multicolored outfit walked up to her.

"Hi there," he said, standing close to Chiana. "You know, you have the most wonderful features. I work for Dallek Enterprises—we run several of the entertainment venues here on Liantac, and you would fit in perfectly with a little 'alien goddesses' show we've got going."

" 'Alien goddesses'?" Chiana repeated with a smile.

"Yes indeed. We've already got three Sebaceans and two Luxans, but a Nebari like yourself would really *make* the show. Why, put you in a nice satin number, and you would blow those other alien females right off the stage. I mean, you have truly phenomenal features! Here," he said, handing Chiana a small chip. "This has all the information—auditions are tonight in the Tirr Hotel, Room 17. Trust me, you're practically a shoo-in."

Taking the chip, Chiana asked, "How much does it pay?"

"Excuse me?"

"The gig. How much?"

"Well," the man said hesitantly, "we can negotiate that after the audition."

"Riiiiight. Well, thank you!" she said with her sexiest smile. "See you tonight."

"I can't wait," the man said, with an expression that Crichton would no doubt have described as "goofy."

Chiana made her way to Stran's Used Parts Emporium, pausing along the way to dump all the free chips—including the one from Speckle-Feathers on the platform—into a garbage disposal.

D'Argo had described the place to Chiana—he had only just arrived when the call from Crichton came to meet at Netoros's office—but his descriptions hadn't prepared her for the reality. *This Stran guy has enough junk to give Rygel a run for his money.*

"Hi there," she said to the man behind the desk as she entered. "You must be Stran."

"Yes, I am. What can I do for you?"

"Oh, any number of things, probably." Chiana sashayed through the path that had been cleared to the back table. "Where did you get all this?"

"Here and there. Here, mostly—sometimes people will trade in old parts for cash when they lose at the Casino. And a lot of this stuff was salvaged from people who didn't believe that the larik particles would *really* harm their ship."

"Learned their lesson the hard way, huh?" Chiana said with a wide, knowing grin.

Stran nodded, returning the grin. "Most people do." The grin then fell. "I certainly did."

"Ooh, sounds like there's a story there," Chiana said, leaning down onto the table so that she had to look up at Stran.

"Not really. I trusted people I shouldn't have trusted, and wound up here. I used to work on ships like this," he said, holding up an engine part that Chiana didn't recognize. "Now I just sell the spare parts."

Gazing into Stran's green eyes, Chiana said, "That sounds like a bit of a come-down."

"You'd think so, but it wasn't, really. I mean, I thought it was when it happened, of course. But hey, I'm making a living. It's not great, but it's enough to keep food on the table."

"I've never been satisfied with that, myself," Chiana said. "I mean, why settle?"

"Well, that's the way things worked out." Stran had gotten a distant look in his eyes, then brought himself back and looked at Chiana. "Anyhow, you didn't come here to hear my life story. I assume you need used parts. Which ones?"

"It's all here," Chiana said, handing him the list that D'Argo had given her.

He looked it over. "This is the same stuff that that Luxan was asking for before."

Chiana nodded. "We're shipmates. He got sucked into some other weird thing, so he sent me along."

"Wait a microt, you're *shipmates*?" He shook his head. "Y'know on this planet, I think I've seen everything. But a Luxan and a Nebari on a ship together—that's new."

Opting not to share the story of just how together this particular Luxan and Nebari had been, Chiana simply said, "Oh, we're a pretty . . . eclectic bunch, you might say. We've also got a Delvian pa'u, a guy from some race nobody's ever heard of, a Hynerian idiot, and an ex-Peacekeeper."

"Ex-Peacekeeper, huh?" Stran said with a chuckle. "I'd like to meet him."

Chiana decided to test a theory. *This little errand is Aeryn's speciality, so how come she's back on Moya?* Chiana hadn't been given an explanation for the changes to the plan, but she had a feeling it had something to do with Stran here, and his interest in meeting an ex-Peacekeeper.

"It's a her, actually. Her name is Aeryn Sun."

Stran straightened up and dropped the list on the table. "Aeryn Sun is your shipmate?"

"Mmm. Why, do you know her?" Chiana asked innocently.

"Yes, I know Officer Aeryn Sun of Pleisar Regiment quite well."

Chiana could have sworn that she felt the temperature in the place drop.

"Remember that career change I mentioned?" Stran said bitterly. "Well, she had a *lot* to do with it. I'm afraid I can't help you."

"What?"

"If you're here with Aeryn Sun, then I'm afraid we can't do business. Goodbye."

"Oh, come on." Chiana leaned in toward him some more. "Don't mess up my life just because you don't like Aeryn. I mean, *I* don't like Aeryn. Nobody does—except Crichton, he likes everybody. But we need that Prowler of hers in good working order. Besides," she said, lowering her voice, "she'll be really upset with me if I don't do this."

Stran put up his hands and closed his eyes. "Wait—wait just one microt." He opened his eyes again and stared at Chiana. "Are you telling me that Officer Sun is on your ship?"

"That's right."

"With you, a Luxan, a Hynerian, a Delvian, and a something else?"

Chiana nodded.

"No Peacekeeper would stand for that!"

"Of course not. I told you, she's an ex-Peacekeeper. They kicked her out."

"Kicked her out?"

"That's right."

Stran stared at her for a moment. Then he laughed. "Oh, that is *too* rich! Aeryn Sun kicked out of the Peacekeepers?" He laughed so hard he had to clutch his belly.

Chiana found his laughter infectious, and joined in.

When he calmed down, Stran said, "Uh—I didn't get your name."

"Chiana."

Nodding, Stran said, "Chiana, thank you. You have made my day—no, my cycle. Oh, it's so nice to know that somewhere in this insane universe there is *justice!*" He grinned. "So let's see what we can do about this list of spare parts that *ex*-Officer Sun needs. Not only that, I'll give you a bargain on whatever you want. After all, we wouldn't want to cheat *ex*-Officer Sun now, would we?" He laughed again.

Chiana smiled. *Oh, I cannot wait to tell the others about this. The look on Aeryn's face alone will be worth it . . .*

Stran went off to collect the parts on the list. Soon enough, he had most of what Aeryn and Crichton were looking for.

"So," he asked as he searched for the remaining items, "how *did* such a mixed bunch wind up on the same ship?"

"Mostly a mutual desire to stay away from the Peacekeepers." Chiana saw no reason to go into detail about her own reasons for being on Moya. Frankly, she wasn't bothered by Peacekeepers one way or the other, as long as they left her alone—something her own conformist-minded race would never do.

"Hmm. Interesting."

To Chiana's surprise, Stran didn't press her for details. Chiana wouldn't have given them in any case, but she had expected him at least to ask.

When all the parts that Stran had were piled on the table, Chiana realized that she would never be able to carry them all. "Don't worry," Stran said when she pointed out her problem. "Delivery is part of the service—either to your hotel or to wherever you've parked."

"Hangar Bay 72."

"Fine." He started entering items into his computer. "By the way, there's something you should probably know."

"Oh?"

"Well, if you want to stay away from the Peacekeepers, anyhow. You may want to make sure you're off this planet sooner rather than later."

"I thought the Peacekeepers declared this place off-limits."

"Oh, officially they have." Stran looked up at her. "But people talk around here. And from what I've heard, the Peacekeepers are coming. Honestly, I thought they had finally arrived when I saw Officer—sorry," he grinned viciously, "*ex*-Officer Sun earlier. If she's no longer Peacekeeper, though, then they haven't. But the word is that one of the Consortium has a deal pending with the Peacekeepers. And if that's true, then this place may be crawling with PK soldiers before too long." He looked back at the computer. "So, will you be paying cash?"

Chiana sighed. "Cash."

The others are not going to be happy to hear this, she thought. *And I was just starting to like this planet.*

CHAPTER 6

ime to go home, I think."

D'Argo's relief at hearing those words from Licit was immense. He was supposed to meet with the others at the hangar bay at midnight. Even if he couldn't be there in person, he at least could participate via comm. That task would be much easier from Licit's home than from the midst of a noisy tavern, and he was worried that Licit would stay at the frelling bar for his "adoring public" all night. They had already been there considerably longer than Licit had promised.

By now the Luxan warrior had sufficiently intimidated people into leaving Licit alone. Between what he did to Tresser and that annoying fan, the patrons gave Licit a wide berth. So now all D'Argo had to do was, as Crichton had put it, stand around and growl a lot.

D'Argo just hoped the whole thing would be over soon. He hated the idea of being a bodyguard, and not just because it was in order to extricate them from a situation of Rygel's devising. The job was too passive. A soldier went out and fought battles. A bodyguard just stood around and waited for battle to come to him. It simply wasn't worthy of his skills.

But then, is anything anymore? he asked himself. As he had said to Aeryn, he wasn't a soldier anymore—hadn't been since the Peacekeepers had framed him for the death of his wife Lo'Laan and separated him from his son Jothee ten cycles ago. Eight cycles as a prisoner, two more as a fugitive. *And now this—being a bodyguard to pay off an Hynerian's gambling debts.*

"Come, Ka," Licit said pleasantly, having lapped up the last of his drink. "Let us be off."

D'Argo winced. Only Lo'Laan had ever called him by his given name. Even his comrades on Moya referred to him by his family name. But after chasing off Tresser, Licit had suddenly reversed his antipathy and decided that D'Argo was a wonderful being and his new best friend. D'Argo wasn't sure which made him more ill, Licit sneering at him or Licit smiling at him.

Ultimately, he decided that Licit just made him ill.

"Much as I am loath to leave my loyal fans," the singer continued, "I must be well rested for tomorrow's shows. Goodnight, all!" he said to the crowd at large, all of whom kept their distance out of respect for D'Argo.

Several fans made noises about how great Licit was as D'Argo led him to the door to the dressing rooms, and thence to the rear exit.

Ah, Lo'Laan, if you could only see me now, D'Argo thought sadly. *But then, if you could see me now, I wouldn't be in this frelling position.*

D'Argo had to admit that there was much about the last two cycles that he did not regret. In Crichton he had found as good a friend as he'd ever had in his life. Aeryn had shown him that he could grow to like and respect a Peacekeeper. Both Chiana and Zhaan had become very important to him as well. Had he not been on Moya, he probably would never have had the opportunity to attend an Orican or see the birth of a Leviathan—even if neither of those experiences had gone at all according to plan.

But I would trade all of it just to see Lo'Laan again.

As they exited the Harilear Club, D'Argo forced himself to focus on the moment. Licit lived in a large apartment at the top floor of one of Netoros's hotels, located a short walk from the club. Netoros and Reis had shown D'Argo the way there, including Licit's private entrance, before bringing him to his charge. This was the part of the evening where Licit would be most vulnerable—out on the concourse, in a place where, unlike in the club, an attacker would have dozens of avenues of escape.

Not that D'Argo truly expected an attack. Netoros, whatever her other flaws, seemed relatively astute. Her assurances that Licit was imagining things were bolstered by D'Argo's own observation: to wit, that Licit was a fool. D'Argo had no trouble believing that the threats were all in Licit's head, fed by his own voracious ego.

"Well, I for one am looking forward to a good night's sleep," Licit said. "Still, I think I'll sleep better for knowing you're there, Ka. Just the fact that I can face tomorrow knowing that Tresser won't be bleating at me is enough to make me—"

"Licit!" cried a voice. D'Argo turned to see a Delvian man standing nearby. "My name is Holkom. Remember it for as long—or as short—as you live."

He held up a clapped-out pulse rifle, of a type the Peacekeepers had abandoned ten cycles ago.

"Get down!" D'Argo cried, tackling Licit.

The yellow bolts of the pulse rifle shot over D'Argo's and Licit's heads as they fell to the ground. A bolt singed one of D'Argo's tentacles, but did not break the skin.

"She left me, damn you!" Holkom said. "It's all your fault!"

He pulled the trigger again, but this time nothing happened. *No surprise there,* D'Argo thought. *He's lucky that old piece of dren doesn't explode in his face.*

"Frell!" Holkom dropped the rifle, and ran off down the concourse.

"Stop!" D'Argo said, getting up and unsheathing his Qualta in one smooth motion.

A crowd began to form. D'Argo noticed the same Sebacean bouncer from the Harilear in its ranks. He'd seemed astute enough when he'd dealt with that idiot fan D'Argo had pushed over. *Not much to go on for a character reference, but it will have to do.* "You! Watch him!" D'Argo bellowed, pointing at Licit, still lying on the ground and looking somewhat stunned.

Without bothering to see if the bouncer actually did what he'd been ordered to do, D'Argo ran after the Delvian.

As he ran, D'Argo thought about what an awful judge of character he was. *Then again,* he thought, *look at what I first thought of Crichton.* Besides which, his judgment about Licit hadn't really been wrong. He may have been correct about the threat to his life. That didn't change the fact that he was still a fool.

D'Argo was grateful that the attacker was Delvian. His smooth blue pate—like Zhaan, Holkom also kept his head shaved—stood out amid the bright lights of the Casino. *I would have lost a Lian in a couple of microts,* D'Argo reflected.

The crowd showed a perplexing lack of interest in getting out of the way of an armed Luxan. D'Argo consistently found himself in logjams of pedestrians and frequently had to shove people aside. He even was tempted to use his Qualta on one or two of them. Luckily, Holkom was slowed down by the crush as well, allowing D'Argo to keep him in sight.

As D'Argo closed in on him, the Delvian ran through an open door.

D'Argo followed.

It was a restaurant. Holkom grabbed empty chairs, food and diners, and threw them to the ground in his wake as he ran toward the back of the restaurant.

Without breaking stride, D'Argo leapt over the chairs and food and stepped over the stunned diners. *Just one shot, and I can end this,* he thought, but he still didn't have a clear line of sight.

Holkom ran into the kitchen. Lians jumped out of the Delvian's way or were knocked aside. One of them tried to grab D'Argo as he rushed by.

"What do you think you're—"

D'Argo shoved the Lian aside. "You're only making things worse!" he said to Holkom.

But the Delvian kept on running. He reached a rear exit just as a Lian female was coming through it. Holkom knocked her over and ran out, slamming the door behind him.

As D'Argo came through the door, he was pelted with a mass of—something. Some of it was solid, some of it was liquid. All of it smelled awful.

The contents of a garbage container littered the ground.

Rotten food and soiled pieces of paper and cloth clung to D'Argo's clothes, skin, tentacles and hair. Even his clavicle rings were encrusted with filth.

Screaming with primal anger, D'Argo fired his Qualta at the fleeing form, but Holkom turned a corner as he did so, and the shot missed.

D'Argo continued to run, almost slipping on a fruit rind that had stuck to the heel of his boot.

Turning the corner, he saw Holkom running and yelling "There's a mad Luxan derelict after me!" at a group of three security officers, who were standing on a corner drinking.

Netoros had told D'Argo that Security enforced the laws in the Casino, and that the badge that she provided for him meant that Security would treat him like one of their own. However, given that the badge was presently covered in gravy and huulo juice, he doubted that they'd take immediate notice.

But he couldn't afford to let the Delvian out of his sight. Which meant he couldn't waste time explaining himself.

Predictably, one of the security officers set down his

drink at the sight of D'Argo and whipped out his sidearm. "Hold it right there, Luxan."

Letting out a snarl, D'Argo continued charging forward, knocking the man down.

The other two went for D'Argo's arms and tried to restrain him. However, he still had his grip on his Qualta rifle which—thanks to the hold the officer had on his right arm—was pointed downwards. So he fired it.

The impact of the rifle's blast against his shin was more than enough to make the Lian let go of D'Argo's right arm.

He then swung the arm around to punch the last officer in the face. He did so, connecting with the officer's beak.

But the officer did not let go.

The first officer got up and held his weapon to D'Argo's head. "Hold it right there," he repeated.

"You blotching trog! I'm Licit's bodyguard, working for Netoros."

"Right, and I'm the head of the bloody Consortium. Pull the other one. Vret, go get that Delvian—we'll need a statement from him."

"Okay, Sergeant."

D'Argo shoved his soiled badge in the sergeant's face. "Look, my badge. That man tried to kill Licit, and threw garbage on me when I chased him."

The sergeant snatched the badge out of D'Argo's hand. "I'll have to find the owner of this—he'll be wanting his badge back, I'm sure. Now I—"

"Oooof!"

That last came from Vret, who had just been punched in the stomach by Holkom and was now down on the ground.

"Frell," the sergeant muttered.

Taking advantage of the distraction, D'Argo knocked the gun out of the sergeant's hand, then shoved the man to the ground. Without a backward glance, he resumed his chase.

"Get back here!" Then the sergeant's footfalls.

So he will give chase as well. Fine. I'll need to turn this dren-sucker in to someone when I catch him. Assuming I don't kill him first.

D'Argo heard the sergeant calling for backup, which told D'Argo everything he needed to know. *This is going to get a lot more complicated.* D'Argo had plenty of faith in his ability to handle three security officers—but a whole platoon of them might be a problem. Especially as he no longer had his badge and had shot one of them.

But after all this, he was not going to let Holkom get away.

Once again, the Delvian ran into a door; once again, D'Argo followed, wiping brown liquid out of his eyes with a dirty hand.

This was another place like the Harilear: a bar with a stage on which entertainment was provided. In this case, however, the entertainment consisted of two stages containing males and females from a variety of species, all in various stages of undress. D'Argo noted that while the male and female dancers were segregated—males on one stage, females on the other—the audience was completely mixed, showing no favoritism towards one stage or the other.

Several members of the audience shot looks at the armed, odiferous Luxan as he entered, but D'Argo ignored them.

Holkom ran onto the stage and grabbed one of the dancers—a Nebari female wearing only a veil. The woman—taller, rounder, and with much more hair than Chiana—looked very frightened, especially once Holkom started waving his gun around.

Where the hezmana did he—? D'Argo wondered, then recognized the gun as being very similar to the one the sergeant had pointed at D'Argo's head. The Delvian had obviously taken it from Officer Vret after punching him in the stomach.

The dancers froze. Gasps and shouts came from all over the room.

"Nobody move or this Nebari loses her pretty little head!" said Holkom.

The Nebari hostage trembled.

"If you harm one hair on her head, Delvian," D'Argo said, "you won't live to regret it."

"You think you scare me, Luxan?"

"Yes. After all, you ran."

"I'm not afraid to die! But not until I kill that pleeking Licit! He's stolen my Srala, and without her my life is over anyway."

Out of the corner of his eye, D'Argo saw the sergeant edge towards the stage, accompanied by a bulky Lian who looked similar to the Lian bouncers in the Harilear Club. D'Argo hadn't noticed the sergeant's arrival, but he had expected it.

"Right. Everyone calm down," the sergeant said.

"Don't come any closer!" Holkom cried.

The sergeant glanced at D'Argo. "So you *were* telling the truth, eh?"

"Of course," D'Argo said.

"We'll sort it all out after we take care of the loony."

Holkom said, "I want him brought here!"

"Who?" the sergeant asked.

"Licit! I want him here so I can kill him!"

"I'm afraid I can't do that, sir." The sergeant started to move closer to the stage.

"If you don't get him, I'm gonna blow her head off!" Holkom pressed the gun against the dancer's head. "You don't think I'll do it? And stop moving!"

"It's not that we don't think you'll do it," the sergeant said, still speaking calmly, but no longer walking forward, "it's just that we can't just bring people here for you to kill. Now if you'll just—"

"Shut up! Just bring him here!"

D'Argo closed his eyes and sighed. *This is getting ridiculous*, he thought.

He looked around. The stage was about a metra off the ground. It looked like a shoddily constructed platform of fake wood.

Transferring his gaze to the Delvian, he saw the gun still at the dancer's head. Beads of sweat dotted her forehead.

Holkom didn't look much better, even considering the fact that Delvians lacked sweat glands. He definitely had what Crichton would call an itchy trigger finger.

D'Argo looked more closely at the gun. Then he sighed.

Lifting his Qualta, he fired at the stage directly under the Delvian's feet.

Before the dancer could fall through the hole, D'Argo leapt onto the stage and grabbed her by the arm.

Holkom, however, found himself sprawled in the hole, dazed.

D'Argo started to guide the dancer to the edge of the stage, but she angrily ripped her arm from his grip and said, "Get the frell off me, you smelly Luxan! Go get yourself a bath or something!"

Perfect, D'Argo thought. *Rygel, you will die for this.*

"What in the name of Thori's bloody beak did you think you were doing?" the sergeant said, as he joined D'Argo on the stage. "He could've discharged the bloody gun when he lost his footing."

"No, he couldn't have," D'Argo said, bending down to pick up the weapon that the Delvian had dropped. He showed the sergeant the gun—with the small red light still on. "He forgot to disengage the safety."

Holkom was muttering. "Left me . . . she left me . . ."

Pointing his gun—with the safety light shining green, meaning it was most definitely disengaged—the sergeant said wearily, "Get up, you bloody piece of dren."

Since Holkom didn't show any sign of moving, D'Argo hauled him up and threw him at the sergeant. "Here."

"Right. Now, you're both coming with me." Before D'Argo could object, the sergeant continued, "You've got to answer some questions—plus you assaulted one of my people. Now, we're going down to the Security office to sort all this out."

"That won't be necessary, Sergeant."

It was Netoros. Standing behind her were the Sebacean bouncer from the Harilear as well a Lian bouncer, both flanking Licit, who huddled between them. D'Argo was surprised to see the singer here—he thought that Licit would get to his apartment as fast as possible and hide under his bed for a few cycles.

"Ka D'Argo is working for me as Licit's bodyguard. Any action he took, he did with my authorization. There is no need for him to accompany you now. Any statement you need from him can wait until morning."

"With all respect—" the sergeant started, but Netoros would not let him complete the sentence.

"Right now I need him to escort Licit home. It's been a very trying evening for him and—"

"This Luxan fired his weapon on one of my officers!" the sergeant said. "And he—"

"As I said, he was working with my authorization. If you wish to make a complaint against one of my employees, you are effectively complaining about me. Is that the case, Sergeant? And be advised," Netoros added, "that that rank of yours is a changeable thing."

The sergeant started to speak, then stopped. Looking down at the club's dark floor he finally said, "I have no complaint against any member of the Consortium."

"Good. See that it stays that way, Sergeant. In the morning, both D'Argo and Licit will give full statements about the attempted murder, along with any other witnesses from my club. You can expect full cooperation from us."

D'Argo tried not to laugh. If Netoros had truly intended to cooperate, she would have let the sergeant take D'Argo with him. Not that D'Argo had any intention of going— right now all he planned to do was bring Licit home, if for no other reason than to have access to the singer's bathroom.

The sergeant led Holkom off, meeting with the backup he'd called, who were waiting outside the club. Netoros escorted D'Argo, Licit, and the two bouncers into a large vehicle with plush interiors.

"Uh, are you sure . . ." Licit murmured as D'Argo sat down in the seat.

"Is there a problem?" D'Argo asked Licit pointedly.

"Ah, no. No problem."

Let them suffer with the smell. Why should I be the only one? D'Argo thought. *Besides, it's not like Netoros can't afford to clean the seats.*

To the driver, Netoros said, "Take us to the Esher."

It was a brief trip to the hotel Netoros owned, but long enough for Netoros to say, "Excellent work, D'Argo. Hopefully this will not only end the death threats to Licit, but deter other fanatics from trying something foolish."

D'Argo said nothing. He didn't care about Licit or the attacks on his person. He just wanted a bath.

At the Esher, Netoros told D'Argo she'd see him in the morning and left with the bouncers. D'Argo and Licit rode the lift to the latter's apartment.

The apartment itself seemed as large as a cargo bay on Moya. It was filled with uncomfortable-looking furniture and tasteless artwork, and though there were no windows, there were plenty of mirrors.

Licit pointed to a door. "In there."

The bathroom he stepped into was as large as D'Argo's quarters. *Whatever Licit's flaws, and there are many,* thought D'Argo, *he does have excellent bathing facilities.*

He spent the better part of an arn in there and emerged feeling much better than he had in a long time.

Although D'Argo's Qualta was right where he had left it on the sink, his clothes had been removed and a dressing gown was left in its place. Unfortunately, it was far too small for D'Argo, so he simply wrapped a towel around himself and exited the bathroom.

"Ah, Ka, good. I've poured you a drink," the singer said as D'Argo came into the living room.

"Where are my clothes?"

"Being cleaned. Don't worry, they'll be as good as new when my valet is through with them."

D'Argo sighed. "Very well." *I suppose I shouldn't have expected otherwise.*

"In the meantime, sit. Let us drink to the successful capture of that Delvian lunatic."

On instinct, D'Argo was going to refuse—he really had no interest in drinking with Licit, or even remaining in his presence any longer than necessary—but he'd had time to think while he was bathing. He remembered what Crichton had said about learning more about the planet and Netoros. Licit worked for Netoros and seemed to be in a voluble mood. *Why not take advantage of it?* D'Argo thought.

So he took the drink—which was poured into a small cup—and sat down on a couch near Licit's chair.

Licit's drink was on a stand connected to the chair's arm. "Let us drink to incarcerated Delvians," he said, and promptly started on his drink.

With a grunt, D'Argo took a sip from his cup. The drink wasn't bad—sweet without being overly sickly, and with a fruity aftertaste.

"So," D'Argo began, in an attempt to elicit some information, "how long have you been working for Netoros?"

"About three cycles now," Licit replied. "I started out playing at the Ordov Club. Dreary little place on the south end of the Casino, but they gave me a break—needed someone to open up for a comedian. People liked me, and I started to develop a small following—but there were limits. Ordov was horrendous at marketing, and he never turned a profit. Finally, he gave up and put the place up for sale. Netoros came in one day to see if she wanted to buy. She saw me, liked what she saw, bought the club, fired everybody attached to it, tore it down, put up a hotel in its place, and hired me to play the Harilear. I started out opening for Thal, believe it or not. That was *quite* a gig. After she retired, I became the headliner. Soon, I was more popular than Thal had been. Netoros brought in Reis to handle my management, and she paid me four times what Ordov was giving me. It was less than I deserved, of course, but it took me a while to realize it. I had stars in my eyes," he added with a chuckle. "Eventually, I made what Thal was making—now I make quite a bit more, of course."

D'Argo had no idea who Thal was, but he was starting

to get a picture of Netoros. 'Netoros always gets what she wants?"

Licit nodded. "Always. The only reason she's on the Consortium is because she wanted some of the laws to change. She thought some of the restrictions were too— ah—restrictive. So she worked her beak off, as it were, to own enough of the Casino to become part of the Consortium, then moved to get the laws changed."

"Impressive," D'Argo said, though he was more disgusted than impressed.

"Oh, she is, she is. She's very good at getting what she wants. She has a place called the House of Games. Very low-key—she likes it that way. Simple little gambling establishment. She's got a Haunan table in the back room that she uses to fleece people."

"How?"

"Oh, the whole bit—duplicate cards, surveillance cameras on the other players, you name it. She controls *every* game on that table, down to the last bet. Sometimes she uses it to curry favor with people by letting them win, or she'll fleece someone who's winning too much. It's pretty amazing. There's even a rumor going around that she has some deal in the works to restore Liantac to its former glory." Licit let out a snort. "I'm not sure I believe that. You can't always trust the gossip of gamblers. Still, if anyone can re-establish this planet, I'm sure it's her. I've learned not to doubt her abilities. She certainly found me an excellent bodyguard." He lapped up some of his drink. "But enough—we were talking about me, not Netoros. I remember one time when I was back at the Ordov, there was this idiot Sheyang—"

Licit continued to drone on about his life as an entertainer, a subject in which D'Argo had no interest. He was, however, very interested in what he'd been told about Netoros, although he was irritated at the realization that Rygel must have been telling the truth about being cheated.

At this point the valet came in. "Excuse me, sir," he told Licit, "but your bodyguard's clothes have been restored."

"Good as new, eh?" Licit asked.

"I am afraid I cannot work miracles, sir, but the items in question have been restored to their former—glory."

D'Argo got up. "Good. I have somewhere I need to be."

"Excuse me?" Licit asked in a surprised tone, looking up at the Luxan. "You're still my bodyguard, Ka. I can't very well—"

"I will return when I am done with my appointment. It is unlikely that you will be needing me here."

"Perhaps, but I'd feel much better—"

"Too bad." Turning to the valet, D'Argo said, "My clothes."

"If you will follow me, sir."

D'Argo followed. *I should introduce this valet to Rygel— they can compete for arrogance.*

CHAPTER 7

S o who are you, exactly, little one?"

Rygel looked up indignantly at the tall, black-feathered Lian. It was Garess, who had finally deigned to exit his office and acknowledge Rygel's existence. The dominar had been hoping to procure information, as Crichton had suggested, but Garess had remained in his office, gabbing away on his comm, making endless business deals. Rygel thought it odd for a person as high ranking as Garess to work so much. *The true art of leadership is delegation,* Rygel reflected. *Otherwise, you don't get to enjoy the fruits of power.*

Crichton had once quoted some idiotic saying from his home planet: "Power tends to corrupt, and absolute power corrupts absolutely."

Rygel had quickly come up with a variation that he much preferred and found to be more accurate: "Power corrupts—what the yotz else is it for, anyway?"

"I know," Garess continued, "that Netoros has prevailed upon your friend Zhaan to help me complete my collection, but I was unaware she was sending me a crippled Hynerian too."

"I am *not* crippled! I am Dominar Rygel XVI of the Hynerian Empire!"

"Ah, I see—not crippled, but lazy," Garess said, giving Rygel's hovering ThroneSled a look of disdain.

"I am a dominar! It is unseemly for me to walk as others do."

"Call it what you like," Garess said dismissively. "In any case, you obviously have no gambling talent to speak of, since you're wearing that collar. Let me guess, Zhaan brought you here to keep you from climbing further into debt? Spiritual types tend to be helpful that way."

Trying to keep his anger under control—it wouldn't do to offend one's host, especially if one wanted something from him—Rygel merely said, "I don't see that that is any business of yours."

Garess laughed. "I'll take that as a yes. The servants have been complaining about you, by the way—they say you've been running them off their feet with your incessant demands for food."

What the yotz else do I have to do in this dreary place but eat? Rygel stopped himself from saying it out loud. Instead he said, "I was not aware that there was a restriction on food to guests."

"The pa'u is my guest; you are hers." Garess seemed to consider the point. "I suppose the hospitality should extend to you as well. Tell me, Dominar, do you always eat every meal as if it were your last?"

"No. I eat every meal as if it were my first."

Garess threw his head back and laughed. "Oh, I *like* you, Dominar. Well, come, let me show you the rest of my abode. I've concluded my business for the time being, and can turn to more pleasurable pursuits."

Rygel chuckled. "About time. If you ask me, for someone who's supposed to be in charge, you spend far too long working."

Leading Rygel around the back area of the dwelling,

Garess said, "This section is my residential space. I don't generally let people back here, except for servants. However, this is also where I have my large storage area, and Zhaan needed to set up back there to do her work. That's why you may have noticed a paucity of decoration."

"Yes, I had noticed. I was going to ask if your decorator was blind."

Garess chuckled. "No, it's simply that my guests don't generally come back here." He walked up to a small door and waved his hand over the sensor.

It opened to a lavish sitting room. *This*, Rygel thought, *is more like it*. Plush furniture sat on the floors in a variety of shapes and sizes to accommodate the needs of a variety of species. Paintings hung from the walls, all looking to Rygel like originals, and ranging in style from Luxan impressionism and Nebari realism to Delvian circular representationalism. Statuary and sculptures were placed about the room. The former included a copy of a large Hynerian piece, a representation of one of the lesser Hynerian gods. Rygel was particularly taken with a collection of Halosian fire crystals in a cabinet next to the sofa. Tables and sideboards were filled with items of obvious value.

All in all, a most heartening example of conspicuous consumption. Rygel approved.

"This is where I generally entertain my guests." His eyes twinkling, Garess turned to Rygel and said, "So, you think I should have servants and assistants and the like performing my duties for me while I lounge about in here and live the good life—or perhaps just flit about in a hovering ThroneSled?"

"Something like that, yes."

"I used to be like that, you know. I had dozens of people at my beck and call—they were my wings that allowed me to fly. The only problem was, eventually they all thought that they could fly on their own. You see, one difficulty with having all this power is that those who work for you tend to get delusions of grandeur."

Rygel thought of his cousin, presently sitting on the

throne that was rightfully Rygel's, and said, "I see your point."

Garess took a seat in one of the large chairs. A servant came in with a drink in a bowl and set it on a small holder on the chair's armrest. "So lately, I've taken to doing it all myself. Besides, I don't work all the time. I go in spurts— nothing but work for several arns at a time, then no work whatsoever for the rest of the day. Works rather nicely, that. Anything for you?"

"If you have any of those huulo fruits left, a plate of them with some cream. And something to wash it down— preferably in a flagon."

The servant nodded and departed.

"I must say," Rygel said, positioning his ThroneSled so he faced Garess, "I find your attitude curious. Micromanaging the day-to-day affairs can lead to madness. Why have the power if you can't enjoy it?"

"Oh, but I do. The thing is—your power is hereditary, is it not?"

"Of course."

"Ah, yes, well, it doesn't work like that here. In order to become part of the Consortium, you must personally own at least ten per cent of the Casino—and at least half of it must be profitable."

"Can't one simply inherit the holdings of a parent?"

Garess stared at him. "I suppose it is possible—if the parent wants to favour one child over all the others, or if he or she somehow outlives all but one offspring. But that's extremely rare."

Rygel remembered that Lian families averaged about a dozen offspring, and they had no tradition of primogeniture. After the parents died, their holdings tended to be distributed evenly among all the children. "Of course, of course. So everyone must build themselves up from the foundation, as it were."

"Exactly. When you've had to work for it, you tend to feel the need to be more hands-on. Who knows? If you'd had to earn your throne instead of being born to it—"

"Are you saying that my cousin deserves to sit on my throne because he somehow 'earned' it by taking it from me?" Rygel said indignantly.

"No, no, no, of course not, Dominar, I misspoke, forgive me." For the first time, Garess sounded conciliatory instead of condescending. Rygel, therefore, accepted his apology without further comment.

The servant returned with a bowl of huulo fruit slices bathed in cream, and a flagon of red liquid. The fruit slices were the deepest purple Rygel had ever seen on huulo fruit, and the cream was just the right shade of blue. He quickly popped several fruit slices into his mouth. *Perfectly ripe.* Then he took a sip from the flagon. The pleasantly bitter wine slid down his gullet. *Good vintage.*

It also served to wash the bitter taste of the conversation out of his mouth. He had to remind himself that he was here to gain information, not to let this yotz get his dander up with his inane posturing about how hard he had to work.

After gulping a few more slices of fruit, Rygel asked, "How did you manage to get such ripe huulo fruit to grow here?"

"Ah, that's perhaps the most fascinating part of this abode." Garess got up. "If you like, I'll show you the arboretum."

Rygel was reluctant to leave before finishing his fruit—then decided he didn't have to. He grabbed the rest of the fruit and stuffed it in his mouth in one go.

"I suppose Hynerian dining customs differ from ours," Garess observed drily.

"Yes, we actually use our hands instead of bending over into the bowl," Rygel replied unperturbed.

Then he leavened his tone with a chuckle. *Remember, Dominar,* he admonished himself, *you don't need to like him, but you do need him to like you.* He continued: "I know what you meant. I'm afraid that being on the run, preceded by hundreds of cycles as a Peacekeeper prisoner, may have dulled my etiquette a bit."

Garess seemed taken aback. His face lost the haughty

expression that it had worn since he first entered Rygel's presence.

"Thori's beak, I had no idea. Hundreds of cycles?"

"Yes." Rygel felt very satisfied to have wiped that look off Garess's face.

"And yet you retain your bearing. I salute you, sir," Garess said with a bow. "Truly, you are of noble blood."

Victory! Now to twist the knife a bit. "Even for an uncouth, lazy, failed gambler?"

Again Garess laughed. "Even for all that, yes. Come, let me show you my passion, and you will understand why I am so grateful for the presence of your friend."

From condescension to friendly tour-guide in less than a quarter arn. You haven't lost your touch, Dominar, Rygel thought with a smile as he washed down the luscious huulo fruit with the wine.

Rygel followed Garess out through an ornate set of old-fashioned wooden double doors that had to be opened manually. Rygel hadn't seen anything that primitive in ages.

The hallways Garess led him through were almost as lavishly appointed as the sitting room, though it was obvious that the latter was the centerpiece of the home. These walls were decorated with more paintings, some of which Rygel recognized. *I wonder how many of them were used to pay off gambling debts,* he mused.

They passed by a huge dining room with a long, oval-shaped table that looked as though it could seat up to fifty. Interestingly enough, this room was not lit by the usual illuminated walls, but by a large chandelier hanging from the ceiling. Rygel had always thought such old-fashioned accoutrements, while admittedly charming, to be unnecessarily dangerous. Why risk crushing your dinner guests with an unwieldy piece of crystal hung only by a single chain when you could provide the same effect with modern technology and no risk?

Unless, of course, you want *to crush your dinner guests,* Rygel reflected, remembering more than one state dinner on Hyneria where that would have been of benefit.

Through one more hallway, then to a large door that had not a sensor, but a coded lock. Garess stood so that his body blocked the buttons onto which he presumably entered a code. Then a light scanned his eyes. *All this for an arboretum.* Rygel scratched himself thoughtfully. *Interesting.*

Rygel wondered how long it would take Chiana to crack the lock.

The door opened. Garess led Rygel down yet another corridor. The sudden humidity in the air took Rygel by surprise.

They turned a corner, and were surrounded by an amazing array of plants. Rygel noticed that none of them overlapped. Then he got closer and saw how it was done: each plant was in a display case made from a flexible casing. The cases' shapes were all molded to accommodate the plants' growth pattern. "Do you replace the cases," he asked Garess, "or just reshape them?"

"They reshape themselves, actually."

Rygel turned in surprise at that. "How?"

"It's a wonderful material that comes from this asteroid in some Luxan colony world or other. The Luxans have an unpronounceable name for it that the translator microbes usually render as gibberish—I just call it the case material. In any event, it works like a liquid in reverse—it conforms to the size of what it's containing—and it's more solid than any metal alloy you can think of. Best of all, it's transparent, so each plant gets the light it needs."

Rygel worked his way down the aisle that had been cleared between the rows of plants. "Not bad," he said. "This is an impressive little—"

He reached the end of the aisle and realized that "little" was the wrong adjective to use. Rygel had assumed that this was the only aisle and that Garess's collection included about a dozen specimens—impressive for a planet with so little vegetation as Liantac. The plants were of sufficient height and Rygel's ThroneSled was presently close enough to the ground that he hadn't really been able to see beyond what was right in front of him.

But when he came to the end of that first aisle, he got a better view of what was past it. Where they came in was only one of about a score of aisles. Each went off in a different direction, each lined with a different set of plants. The arboretum, he realized, was larger than the rest of the whole house—possibly larger than Moya's biggest cargo bay.

The plants that flowered came in as many colors as some of the Casino signs, and the leaves were glorious shades of purple, blue, green, red and gold. Down one aisle, he saw a good-sized huulo bush that was equal parts bright green with leaves and bright purple with fruit.

"I've never seen an arboretum with so many plants." Rygel said with a chuckle. "Come to think of it, I don't think I've ever seen so many plants anywhere."

"I love plants," Garess said with a dreamy look. He went on, speaking with a reverence that belied his earlier tone. "Ironic, since I grew up on a world where most of the plant life has been wiped out, aside from what's in preserves, but I've been obsessed with them all my life. Who knows, perhaps it's because this world's flora has been so decimated. In any case, I love the colors, watching them grow—it's truly beautiful." He sighed. "So little on this world is naturally beautiful. So much is created. So much is artificial. But *this*," he said with a gesture towards their surroundings, "this is *real*. This is *true* beauty! And now that the pa'u is here, I have at least one sample of every known plant from this area of space."

Rygel turned in surprise. "*Every* one?"

"Admittedly, there are always new plants sprouting up—so to speak—" the twinkle returned to Garess's eye as he said it, "—but I think I can say with certainty, that these last fifteen plants will make my collection complete."

As Garess guided Rygel through the arboretum, he quoted chapter and verse on each plant—its special features, from whom he acquired them, and so on. And on and on.

Rygel might have been able to feign interest more convincingly if it weren't so frelling humid. His tunic was sticking to his chest, and his rear end was slipping on the cushion of his ThroneSled.

Garess then showed Rygel the fifteen containers intended to hold the samples that Zhaan was going through right now. The case material was perfectly symmetrical and cylindrical on these. Rygel presumed that that was the default shape it maintained while waiting for an item to be placed within its confines. He noticed that one of them had an attachment. Unlike whatever Garess was droning on about, this was something that genuinely sparked Rygel's curiosity, and he asked, "Why is that one different?"

"Oh, this is for a specimen that needs to be in stasis. It cannot possibly thrive in the environment of the display cases otherwise."

"Wrong climate, eh?"

"Something like that, yes."

Garess then proceeded to explain about some of the other plants he had in stasis besides whatever the new one was. Rygel was wondering how he could change the conversation of this infinitely dull topic back to the Consortium, and possibly thence to Netoros, when a servant suddenly appeared, as if from nowhere. Rygel silently approved of his unobtrusiveness. Servants were best when they weren't obvious.

"Excuse me, sir, but you have an urgent call from the head of the construction firm. There has been some sort of crisis with the refurbishing of the luxury hotel suites. I tried to explain that you were not taking calls, but she insists on speaking to you."

Garess sighed. "Unfortunately, I *did* tell her to contact me directly if there was a problem, regardless of the time of day. Stay with the dominar until he's finished his tour and lock up behind him please, Arco." He turned to Rygel. "My apologies, Dominar, but I must deal with this. Feel free to stay in the arboretum as long as you like."

That should be about a half a microt, Rygel thought, squirming in his ThroneSled and dabbing sweat from his brow. He waited for Garess to depart, then turned back to the aisle they had come in through. Arco followed silently behind.

Once Arco locked the door behind them, Rygel said to the servant, "I will be with the Delvian. Bring me another bowl of that wonderful huulo fruit in cream."

Arco simply nodded and went toward the kitchen. Rygel navigated his way through the lush rooms and halls of the public part of the house and into the drearier residential area.

Zhaan sat at a metallic table in Garess's massive storage area, surrounded by a huge variety of plastiform containers that had some kind of electronics attached to them—ones much larger than the stasis attachment Rygel had seen in the arboretum. Zhaan had explained earlier that the containers regulated the atmosphere for transport so the flora could survive the changing conditions. Rygel wondered why they weren't all just in stasis, which seemed to be less complex, but he didn't care enough to actually ask the question. *I'll probably get an answer that will take two arns*.

The good news for Rygel was that this storage area was spared the oppressive humidity of the arboretum, for which he was quite grateful. The table also held seven different analysers. Rygel didn't have a clue as to how they worked, but Zhaan operated each of them with practiced ease. Occasionally, she consulted a computer that sat nearby.

"Hello, Rygel," Zhaan said. She was moving the smallest of the analysers over a small brown branch.

"Enjoying yourself, I hope," Rygel said.

Laughing, Zhaan replied, "Yes, immensely. You're bored to tears, I assume?"

"I've had more exciting times in my life. It won't be long before we're to meet at the hangar."

"I'm afraid I shall have to decline—I'll participate via comm, but I'm having trouble identifying this one tree. I *think* it's a Vorcarian flytrap, but it might be a—"

Holding up one hand, and putting the other to his head, Rygel said in a pleading voice, "Zhaan, I've already listened to Garess wax eloquent about his frelling plants. I don't need you doing it, too."

Zhaan looked up. "You've spoken to Garess?"

"Yes, he finally graced me with his munificent presence," Rygel said scornfully. "He started a tour of the house, then took me to the arboretum where your new companions will wind up soon."

Zhaan chuckled. "They're hardly my companions, Rygel. And I hope I can get that tour myself. I'd love to see what Garess has displayed. According to Netoros, he has quite a collection."

" 'Quite a collection' doesn't begin to cover it. I've been in sparser forests. In fact, he says that once your samples are catalogued, he'll have one of every known plant. Or so he *claims*, anyhow."

"Anything's possible," Zhaan said with another smile. "Now if you'll excuse me, I must get back to this Vorcarian flytrap—or whatever it is."

Arco came in with another bowl of fruit.

"Ah, excellent," Rygel said, steering his ThroneSled to where Arco stood and holding out his hands. "I'll take that."

Silently and carefully, Arco handed Rygel the bowl, making sure the cream didn't slosh over the side. *This is excellent fruit*, Rygel thought to himself. *It would've been worth hearing Garess's entire lecture for more of this. Wonder if I can talk him into trading some when we finally get away from this place.*

As he ate, Rygel watched Zhaan toiling away. *The amazing thing is, she's enjoying herself.* Rygel had always thought it odd that Zhaan, who like all Delvians was vegetable rather than animal, would take such an interest in plants. *Then again, I've encountered my share of animal lovers as well.*

Tossing some more fruit into his gullet, he thought, *I'd*

much rather be trying to get my winnings back right now.
A few more Haunan games, and I'd not only get Moya
back, but all those ferries of theirs as well.

He gazed at the containers, wondering how many retri
Garess had wasted on them. Rygel understood the collector
mentality, but what was so interesting about plants?

He popped the last huulo into his mouth and then drank
down the cream, spilling some on his robe and staining it
blue. *I suppose the collection as a whole is worth something*
just by dint of having every plant in the—

Then he noticed something odd. He counted the containers in the storage area and realized that they only numbered
fourteen. But there had been fifteen display cases in the
arboretum, and Garess had made reference to fifteen samples. Rygel was sure of it.

As sure as he had been that Steen had been dealt the
fourth king.

"Zhaan?"

"Yes, Rygel?" the priest said, so intent on her task that
she didn't even look up at him.

"Are there any other samples?"

"What do you mean?"

"Are these fourteen the only ones?"

"Yes," Zhaan replied. "Why?"

"Because Garess has *fifteen* empty sample cases in the
arboretum. Because one of those cases had an attachment
that puts whatever's inside it in stasis. Because Garess's
precise words were, 'And now that the pa'u is here, I have
at least one sample of every known plant from this area of
space.' And because I didn't see any Delvians in display
cases in the arboretum."

Zhaan turned a very pale shade of blue.

Aeryn loved the quiet.

That, at least, was what she tried to tell herself.

She certainly thought she had been looking forward to
it. No D'Argo bellowing, no Zhaan making cryptic statements, no Chiana getting underfoot, no Rygel being ob-

noxious and, best of all, no Crichton trying to reconstruct lyrics to idiotic human songs. While on Liantac with its endless stream of noise, all she had dreamt of was being somewhere quiet again.

With everyone down on Liantac, she now had her wish. All was quiet on Moya.

So why am I so frelling jumpy?

She found herself suppressing an urge to scream, just so there would be some noise. But there was nothing except for the usual background noise made in the course of normal operations. But Aeryn hardly counted that. She'd spent all her life on spacefaring vessels; the only time she noticed such noise was when it was absent.

The silence gave her the space to think. *And, as D'Argo so astutely pointed out, I don't like to think.* Aeryn was a creature of action, not thought. Peacekeepers weren't encouraged to think, save when it related to duty.

Except, of course, her thoughts right now were related to duty. Or, at least, her former duties.

Technician Eff Stran was still alive, and he, understandably, despised her.

For some reason, he hadn't killed her when he'd had the chance—he'd merely let her walk away. *If I had been in his place, I'm not sure I'd have been so merciful.*

But then, in a sense, I am in his place. Perhaps I should go back down there, explain things to him.

Aeryn let out a laugh. *Oh, I'm sure he'll take to that. "Oh, you're not a Peacekeeper anymore? Well, that's all right, then. Come, let's go for a drink, and I'll just forget about how you were responsible for reducing me to running a used parts emporium after spending all my life as a respected Peacekeeper tech."*

No, her best bet was to remain on Moya until this nonsense was over and done with.

She wandered to Pilot's den. Aeryn had always preferred to speak to him face to face. Perhaps because she, too, was a pilot, she understood the importance of his role. Although she'd never been symbiotically linked to any of her ships, she knew the close relationship that developed between flyer and vessel, and knew that Pilot was easily the most important person on Moya.

The massive door to the den swivelled open. "What's the status, Pilot?"

Pilot's four arms moved easily across the various consoles in front of him as he looked up at Aeryn. "Some of Moya's systems are acting—peculiar."

Aeryn frowned. Pilot rarely used such imprecise language. "Peculiar how?"

"Difficult to ascertain. So far it's simply that certain systems are responding more slowly than others. The DRDs are investigating further, but sensors aren't detecting anything abnormal."

"Hmm. Well, keep me posted on that, just in case. I—"

"We're picking up a distress call," Pilot interrupted. "It's coming from a ship that's on an orbital approach to Liantac."

"If they're approaching a planet with this many larik particles in orbit, no wonder they're in distress," Aeryn muttered.

Pilot looked at Aeryn. "It isn't an inorganic vessel, Officer Sun—Moya identifies it as one of Liantac's technoorganic ferries."

"Well then it's Liantac's problem. Ignore it." Aeryn moved as if to leave, then stopped as she felt the deck under her shift almost imperceptibly. "Where are we going?" she asked, whirling back to Pilot.

"Moya is moving to intercept the ship and wishes me to make contact."

"It's not our problem, Pilot. Tell her to ignore it. We got into this mess out of a misguided sense of altruism, I'm not about to let us make that mistake again."

Manipulating more controls, Pilot said, "I am conveying that to Moya, but she will not listen. She feels a certain kinship with the ferries, and will not simply ignore one in distress." Pilot looked down at a readout. "The ferry's captain says he wishes to speak to us."

Much as Aeryn had come to care for Moya, there were times when she preferred a ship that didn't have a mind of its own. "Fine, I'll be in the Command and I'll talk to him there."

She headed to the Command, at once grateful and annoyed. Annoyed that Moya wouldn't take her advice, but grateful that at least she was *doing* something.

And it wasn't quiet anymore.

Aeryn hated the quiet.

"On screen, Pilot," she said as she entered the Command.

The image of the ferry was on the screen—a vessel about the size of Crichton's module, but pink and fleshy. In some ways, it looked even more alive than Moya—perhaps because the hull was almost the same color as Sebacean skin.

Then the image changed to the interior of the ship, and the chaos that Aeryn saw was one she was sadly familiar with: the cockpit of a ship that was falling apart. A Lian was at the controls, and Aeryn could tell by his expression that he was trying desperately to hold things together. The walls and the console were mostly the same shade of pink as the hull, with equally pink protrusions, some of which he was manipulating. Someone was sitting in a chair behind him, but Aeryn couldn't see the passenger very well at this angle.

What was most distressing were the parts of the wall that weren't pink, but an unfortunate shade of brown. It almost looked like rust. Crichton had mentioned that the Lians had been having problems with the ferries rotting—now Aeryn was getting to see the process first-hand. The brown patches were visibly spreading.

"Whoever you are, this is Liantac Ferry 7 requesting immediate assistance."

"What is the nature of your emergency?" Aeryn asked.

"Well, you can see what's wrong, can't you? The damn ship's rotting away! I was promised that they'd solved this problem, which just goes to show you how much you can trust people these days. In any case, I've got a very im-

portant passenger here. She's a Peacekeeper officer, and if I don't—"

Aeryn had been about to interrupt when the ship did it for her. One of those brown patches spread far enough for a hole to open.

The air inside the ferry followed its natural tendency to move to an area of lesser pressure, with the effect of blowing everything inside the ferry toward that hole—including the pilot and the Peacekeeper. Aeryn could see the officer now—she was a red-haired female wearing the uniform of a regimental lieutenant.

The pilot was trying to hold onto the ship by gripping the edges of the hole, but it was a losing battle. The rotting flesh of the ferry was difficult to get a grip on, and the hole was widening, speeding up the decompression process.

Then the screen went blank.

"We have lost communications," Pilot reported, his face appearing in holographic form. *"Moya is continuing her intercept course."*

Aeryn shook her head. "Don't bother, Pilot. There's no chance of saving them. Besides, a Peacekeeper coming here cannot possibly be good for us. Best to just let them die."

"Moya shares your feelings for the Peacekeepers, Officer Sun, but she is concerned with the ferry. Although non-sentient, it is still a fellow bio-mechanoid. She will not just abandon it. The docking web is taking it in."

Sighing, Aeryn replied, "All right, fine, I'll go down and greet them."

Grabbing her pulse rifle, Aeryn headed for the hangar. She was not about to face a Peacekeeper officer unarmed. *If she gives me even the slightest reason, I'll blow her frelling head off.*

As soon as atmosphere was restored to the hangar, Aeryn entered, pulse rifle raised.

She almost dropped the weapon when the smell hit her nose. She hadn't encountered a stench this bad since she'd been sent on a mission to board a runaway garbage scow that had been careening into a Peacekeeper-controlled moon. "Pilot, is that smell coming from the ferry?"

"Yes. The decay is spreading."

"I can see that," Aeryn muttered as she took a closer look at the ferry. The rot she'd seen inside had spread so far that there was more brown than pink on the ship's outer surface.

The Lian pilot was sprawled over the threshold of a hatch. *No, that's not a hatch, that's a hole,* Aeryn realized. Probably the same hole that had opened while Aeryn was talking to him, it was now big enough to accommodate two people walking side by side through it.

Aeryn turned around and looked down at the sound of a familiar whirring noise. One of the DRDs had entered. "Pilot, have the DRD check the Lian for life signs." She didn't want to lower her weapon to do so herself and leave herself defenseless against the Peacekeeper.

"Of course."

The DRD rolled up to the Lian's body and extended some kind of protrusion from its squat, round yellow body. After a moment, the protrusion retracted and Pilot said, *"The Lian is dead."*

Then Aeryn heard movement. Aiming her rifle at the noise, she said, "Come out with your hands where I can see them, Lieutenant."

The Peacekeeper stumbled into sight from round the other side of the ferry. Blood matted her hair and stained her right cheek and most of the right side of her uniform, which was ripped and torn in several places. Her right arm hung uselessly at her side, but she held a large pistol in her left hand. She started to raise the weapon.

"Put it down," Aeryn said in a tight voice. *Just give me one excuse,* she thought.

The lieutenant lowered her arm, then collapsed on the deck, her pistol clattering to her side.

Aeryn knelt, activated the safety on her pulse rifle, set it behind her and out of the Peacekeeper's reach, and then picked up the pistol and held it to the lieutenant's head.

There's only one way I'm going to get any information

out of her, Aeryn thought. "I'm Captain Aeryn Sun, in command of this Peacekeeper prison transport. What is your mission here, Lieutenant?"

Haltingly, she replied, "I am—Lieutenant Clow Asmat—Plexico Company—Me-Medinnus Regiment. I—have—im-important—Peacekeeper business on—Liantac. You must—get me to—to Netoros."

Aeryn knew little of Plexico Company beyond their existence, and even less of Medinnus Regiment—and what she did know was two cycles out of date in any case. She was more interested in the mention of Netoros. "What is your business with the Consortium?"

"No—Consortium—just Netoros—must complete—negotiations with—with—"

Asmat closed her eyes. Aeryn nudged her neck with the pistol and barked, "Stay awake, Lieutenant! What negotiations?"

The DRD moved towards Asmat's still form.

"Answer me!"

"She cannot hear you," Pilot said. *"According to the DRD, Lieutenant Asmat is dead."*

"Damn."

"I am afraid your response confuses me, Officer Sun."

"I don't mourn Lieutenant Asmat's death, Pilot, I just wished she'd timed it better. If she had a meeting with Netoros, I think there's a good possibility that it had something to do with us. I knew there would be more to this than simply settling a debt. Asmat was probably here to take D'Argo, Rygel and Zhaan in—and me, for that matter."

"Probably not you," Pilot said. *"She didn't recognize your name."*

"Or she was so delirious she didn't make the connection. Or perhaps Netoros didn't give her details. We can't risk it. Is it almost midnight planetside?"

"Another quarter of an arn," Pilot said.

"Good," Aeryn said. "It looks like we're going to have a lot to talk about."

CHAPTER 8

Crichton was looking forward to the meeting outside the
hangar. He had great news that he couldn't wait to
share with his crewmates.

He had arrived to find Rygel and D'Argo waiting. Chiana
had arrived a few microts later, having supervised the load-
ing of the merchandise from Stran's Used Parts Emporium
into the transport pod. Aeryn and Zhaan had been contacted
on the comms, and Crichton had been all ready to give his
news.

Except D'Argo had insisted on going first. Well, actually,
Chiana had insisted that D'Argo go first, mainly because
she had heard tell of the capture of Licit's stalker, which
was all anyone on the monorail back from Stran's could
talk about, and Chiana had wanted details. So D'Argo had
provided them, in impressive detail, and had also shared
the relevant parts of his conversation with Licit afterward.
He had ended his tale with the reluctant admission that
Rygel may well have been telling the truth about being
cheated.

Rygel had, of course, gotten his dander up on that subject *again*, but nobody had been interested in hearing an "I told you so." They had, however, been quite interested in Rygel's theory that Garess planned to add Zhaan to his collection of exotic plants once she was finished identifying the others Garess had collected—and also that Rygel was getting on the good side of another member of the Consortium.

Then Chiana had insisted on speaking, first filling everyone in on what she had learned about Rari: that he had specifically left Liantac to rendezvous with a Luxan trader in order to find some "important people." As if that wasn't enough, she had then spoken of the rumor that Stran had heard about a possible Peacekeeper presence on Liantac very soon. D'Argo had added that Licit had heard similar rumours.

Finally, Crichton got a word in.

"I think I found a way to get ships to function even with the larik particles."

"Really?" Chiana said, sounding surprised.

"Don't look so damn shocked—this *is* what I do for a livin,' y'know? Anyhow, it was really simple once I figured it out. See, I realized that the intake—"

"*Crichton,*" Aeryn interrupted, "*much as we'd love to hear all about how brilliant you are, we have more pressing concerns. I'm afraid that the rumors that D'Argo and Chiana heard are true.*"

Aeryn then told everyone about Lieutenant Asmat.

And now I'm completely depressed, Crichton thought.

"*I did warn you all that Netoros might try something like this behind our backs,*" Aeryn said.

"No," Rygel said.

"What do you mean 'no'?" D'Argo asked indignantly.

"I mean that this isn't a simple case of Netoros wishing to turn us in to the Peacekeepers. Zhaan was correct earlier—the reward for our capture alone is not enough to entice Netoros. And she can't possibly have summoned this Asmat woman in the time that we've been here."

Crichton nodded. "Spanky's right, this is way more complicated than just trying to nail us. Sounds like Netoros has some other big plan in mind."

"Then what do we do about it?" D'Argo asked.

Chiana's head tilted. "Why do anything? Who cares what Netoros has going with the Peacekeepers? Let's just do what we're supposed to do and leave."

"It won't be that simple," Rygel said. "Whatever negotiation this Asmat woman of Aeryn's is supposed to carry out will probably have something to do with us. First Netoros brought us here, now she's contrived a way to keep us here. I'll wager that she's going to turn us in to the Peacekeepers as part of whatever deal she's got going with them."

"Your track record with wagers is hardly one hundred percent, Rygel," Aeryn said drily.

"The point is," D'Argo said, "we're being used. I, for one, don't appreciate it."

"For once, the Luxan and I are in total agreement," Rygel said.

"That's the scariest thing I've heard all day," Chiana muttered.

"What we need is more information," Crichton said. "I mean, great, we know that Netoros set us up, but we don't have any proof."

Zhaan added, *"And even if we did, to whom would we report that proof? Netoros is an authority on this planet."*

"Yeah, well, so's Garess," Crichton said. "Rygel, you've been getting in on his good side, right?"

"Yes."

"Good. Keep it up. And be ready for his move against Zhaan. One way or another, we might be able to actually get the upper hand on him—or at least get him on our side."

"That is not an individual I want on my side, John," Zhaan said.

"A Delvian's gotta do what a Delvian's gotta do, Zhaan," Crichton said. "What we need now is information and leverage. Right now, Netoros has all of it."

Chiana smiled. "Not all of it."

Frowning, Crichton asked, "What do you mean, Pip?"

"We have a Peacekeeper negotiator. And Netoros doesn't know that we have her."

"Asmat is dead, Chiana," Aeryn said, *"She's hardly of any use to us."*

"They don't know that," Chiana said, her smile getting wider. "Grab her ident chip, put on her uniform, and finish what she started."

"That's insane."

"Actually," Crichton said, "it's brilliant."

"Thank you," Chiana said, with a slight bow.

"It won't work," Aeryn said. *"For one thing, Asmat's uniform is a total loss, and she's of a completely different build."*

"Then use the lieutenant's uniform you wore when we pulled one over on Larraq last year," said Crichton. "That fits fine."

"You also proved then," D'Argo added, "that you can impersonate a Peacekeeper convincingly."

Crichton knew that was true. Aeryn's impersonation of a Peacekeeper lieutenant had been a great deal more convincing than Crichton's own attempt to impersonate a captain. His failure had almost done them in.

"It's not the impersonation of a Peacekeeper that I'm concerned about," Aeryn said, though Crichton heard a catch in her voice that indicated to him that she was very much concerned about it. *"It's impersonating* this *Peacekeeper. I have no idea what she's supposed to be negotiating, what the terms are, or even if Netoros has met Asmat before. I can't even begin to think of the number of things that can go wrong."*

Grinning, Crichton said, "It's a gamble, Aeryn."

"A big one."

"Well, what better place for that than a gambling planet?"

"That isn't funny."

"Maybe not," said Crichton, "but it's our best chance of

getting the upper hand on Netoros. Meantime, I'll stall her and say I haven't figured out this problem yet. They've waited thirty cycles, they can wait another day or two. Zhaan, you should probably do the same with your little task, since Garess probably won't try to stick you in the cage until you've done everything else."

"Of course."

Pilot's voice came on over the comm. *"I'm sorry to interrupt, but there is a new development. Several of Moya's systems have been acting oddly. The problems have been getting worse, and we're now detecting a pattern—the slow response times we're seeing are consistent with the effects of larik particles."*

D'Argo looked sharply at Crichton. "I thought larik particles didn't affect organic ships."

"They shouldn't," Crichton said. "Pilot, I've spent the last several arns living, eating, and breathing larik particles—a Leviathan's immune system should take care of them with no problem."

"There is one possible explanation," Pilot replied. *"The Clorium field's anaesthetizing qualities might be adversely affecting Moya's immune system. For the moment, we can compensate for the difficulties. But the problems will continue to worsen the longer we remain trapped within this Clorium field."*

"Assuming that is the problem," D'Argo said.

"Yes."

Crichton sighed. "And the hits just keep on comin.' All right—Pip, you'll have to bring the supplies up to Moya, and then stay with her while Aeryn comes down here to play the big, bad PK."

Chiana tilted her head. "Wait a microt, why do *I* have to stay trapped on Moya? I *like* it down here—I'm probably the only one who does right now."

D'Argo muttered, "That much is certain."

Crichton put his hands on Chiana's shoulders. "I know that, Chiana, but we can't just leave Moya alone, especially now, and the rest of us are stuck down here."

"Unless you want to take over bodyguarding Licit," D'Argo added, with a smile.

"Very funny," Chiana said with a pout.

The look brought back memories to Crichton of his sister as a teenager when his dad wouldn't let her go to a party, or borrow the car, or provided some other affront against life and limb that fathers always inflict on teenage girls. *Sometimes I forget just how young Pip is,* he thought.

To his horror, Crichton found himself saying exactly the same thing Dad always said back then: "Please, try to understand and don't fuss, okay?"

The pout faded. "All right—but when this is all over, you owe me a sunset at Terisears's. Deal?"

Presuming that a sunset was a drink and that Terisears's was a bar, Crichton smiled and said, "Deal."

"And I want to make a few stops before I head back into orbit."

"We can't afford—" Aeryn started, but Chiana wouldn't let her finish.

"It's not like anything's going to happen until morning anyhow, Aeryn. You can go down at sun-up, and give me a chance to enjoy myself tonight."

"Fine," Aeryn conceded grumpily.

"I suppose I should go back to that yotz Garess's place, then," Rygel said. "I still say that my talents would be much better served by trying to win back our losses at the Casino."

In perfect unison, Crichton, D'Argo, Aeryn, Zhaan, and Chiana all said, *"No!"*

Rygel's ears drooped. "Very well."

"I will continue to guard Licit and see if I can glean any more useful information from him," D'Argo said.

Grinning, Crichton said, "Yeah, he probably thinks you're the coolest cat around now."

"The feeling is *not* mutual."

"Buck up, D'Argo," Crichton said, giving him a light, friendly punch to the shoulder. "You'll do fine."

"Assuming I don't kill him first."

"If you are forced to kill him, D'Argo," Zhaan said, *"at least be discreet and dispose of the body properly."*

D'Argo laughed at that. "I assume I can count on all of you to aid me if that should come to pass."

"Hey, you know the old saying, D'Argo," Crichton said. "Friends help you move, real friends help you move bodies."

"It's getting late, Pa'u."

Zhaan whirled around. Garess had entered the storage area without making a sound. *Or,* she amended, *no sound that I noticed while I was so engrossed in my work.* She needed to be wary of that . . .

"Did I frighten you?"

"You merely startled me."

"Well, in any case, it *is* getting late, and I was concerned that you would work yourself into a stupor. How is it coming along?"

"Slowly but surely," Zhaan said, switching the analyser off. "I thought this latest sample was a Vorcarian flytrap, but it turned out to be a variant—still Vorcarian, but a more timid plant."

"Is it a fozee?" Garess asked. At Zhaan's affirmative nod, he said, "Good. I was hoping that would be the case— fozees are quite rare."

"Indeed."

"I'm afraid most of the specimens are like that—variants of more common flora. That's why I needed someone like you. While I am as knowledgeable as any amateur could be in such things, I don't know enough to make the precise identifications that you are capable of."

"You could very easily, Garess. You certainly have the appropriate equipment."

"Yes, but what I lack is the time to learn how to use it properly. Perhaps some day I shall retire and devote myself completely to the pursuit. But for now, the pull of business is a great one indeed. So are you going to sit here all night, or can I have Arco show you to your room?"

"Oh, a room is not necessary," Zhaan said. She certainly didn't want this individual's hospitality, particularly if the suspicions she and Rygel had were correct.

"Please, I insist. My guest rooms are finer than the most luxurious rooms in the Casino. I can hardly expect you to try to seek out accommodation at this hour."

"I already have—"

"Nor can I allow you to walk unaccompanied in the Casino this late. There are unsavory elements—as it is, I fear for that poor Hynerian royal."

"Rygel can take care of himself. As can I."

Inclining his head slightly, Garess said, "Of that I have no doubt, Pa'u—still, you are my guests. I insist on being allowed to extend my hospitality to you for the evening so you can get a fresh start on the remaining samples in the morning. I have a room that will be quite comfortable for you—plenty of light."

"Is there—privacy?"

"What do you mean?"

What would be a convincing lie? Zhaan thought quickly. "I am a very—private person, Garess. I cannot be disturbed while meditating. If you can guarantee that I will be able to lock my door, and that only I will be able to open it, then I will take you up on your kind offer."

Garess didn't hesitate. "Of course. You will enter your own code to control the lock. We are very security conscious on Liantac, Pa'u. I can assure you that no one will be able to enter your room once you lock it—not even me."

Zhaan looked Garess in the eyes. He seemed sincere in this statement. But then, he did need Zhaan to finish the work. He was correct in that the samples were all odd, rare variations of more common flora, and the work was indeed tricky. Zhaan probably wouldn't have been able to make the proper identifications without this equipment. But she also knew the right questions to ask of the equipment, as it were, which few on this arid planet would.

"Very well, I accept," she said, forcing a smile.

"Excellent," Garess said. "Well, if there's anything you need, anything at all, don't hesitate to ask me or one of the staff. We want you to be as comfortable as possible."

He moved toward the door, then stopped and turned back to Zhaan. "I want to thank you, Pa'u. Your presence here has truly been a boon to me. I've been wanting to complete my collection for some time, and your arrival has finally allowed me to do that. Words cannot describe how grateful I am."

With that, he left.

Zhaan turned the analyzer back on, stared at it, then turned it back off.

Words may not be able to describe it, Garess, but I suspect your actions will soon enough.

Zhaan thought back on the long cycles of imprisonment that she had had to endure since she murdered her lover in an attempt to keep Delvia away from Peacekeeper influence. True, she had come out of those cycles as a priest, but the benefits hardly outweighed the negative aspects. While she did not feel quite as strongly as, say, D'Argo on the subject of being imprisoned again, she was nevertheless in no rush to repeat the experience.

I will be ready for you, Garess. Goddess grant me the wherewithal to do what needs to be done when the time comes.

CHAPTER 9

Netoros, there's a female here to see you."

Frowning, Netoros turned away from the report from her security staff and looked down at her intercom. "Does she have an appointment?" she asked, already knowing the answer was no. When Netoros came into the office less than an arn ago, Celong had specifically said that there were no visitors on the list for this morning.

"*No,*" Celong said calmly, "*but she has a very large gun, the muzzle of which is distressingly close to my face at present.*"

Netoros blinked. "Excuse me?"

"*She has a very large gun pointed at me. She's also wearing the uniform of a Peacekeeper.*" Celong may as well have been discussing the latest profit statements for all the agitation her voice betrayed at this state of affairs.

The light dawned on Netoros. "Is her name Asmat?"

She heard another voice in the background. "*Yes, Netoros, I'm Lieutenant Asmat, now tell this frelling idiot to let me in.*"

"Let her in, Celong."

"Of course, Netoros."

The door opened, and Celong led in a trim Sebacean with long black hair that framed her angular face. Her penetrating, dark eyes seemed to take in everything at once. She was coiled, ready to spring at a moment's notice. Netoros found her more than a little off-putting.

Celong was still a picture of calm, and Netoros admired her composure. *I don't think I'd be so serene if a Peacekeeper pointed a gun at me,* she thought. *Especially this one. It's going to be a challenge just being in the room with her.*

"It's good to finally meet you," Netoros said, standing and putting her hand on the Sebacean's shoulder.

The lieutenant just gave the hand a disdainful look. Netoros quickly removed it.

"Shall we get on with it?" Asmat asked, sitting in one of the guest chairs.

"Of course. Can I get you something to drink?"

"No, thank you. I'm here to do business. I'd just as soon get it over with."

Taking her seat facing the Peacekeeper, Netoros said, "Pursuant to that, I'd been expecting you sooner. What delayed you?"

The lieutenant shot Netoros a disgusted look, which, if anything, made her even scarier. "The ferry that escorted me. Or almost did, at any rate. It rotted away as we approached this place, and the pilot didn't make it. I only survived because we were towed in by that Leviathan in orbit. So I—borrowed their transport pod and came down." Asmat's tone indicated that she didn't so much borrow as commandeer the vessel.

Netoros nodded her head. "It's ironic, that."

"How?" Asmat asked harshly.

"That Leviathan you encountered is part of our negotiation."

Asmat raised an eyebrow. "Explain."

"Simple. From the beginning, you have expressed displeasure at the lack of short-term benefits for the Peace-keepers in this deal."

"Yes, that has been a concern."

Netoros nodded. "I can understand that. After all, five per cent of our profits may not seem like a great deal. But what you don't understand is that, with your investment, we will finally be able to make Liantac great again."

"I want fifteen per cent."

Netoros blinked. "Excuse me?"

"You heard me. Liantac's economy is in free fall. For as long as those larik particles are up there, nobody can get here except on your wretched ferries."

Netoros raised a finger. "Ah. That brings us to the other benefits. First of all, we will provide you with the specifications for the techno-organic ferries."

Asmat laughed derisively. "What possible use would we have for *those*?"

"Quite a bit if you have a financial stake in the success of Liantac. You have technicians, shipbuilders, engineers and the like. We are successful businesspeople, but the past thirty cycles have proven that we are very bad shipbuilders. Nobody can figure out why the ferries rot, any more than they can determine how to get rid of the larik particles. But you have the resources, and now you have a reason."

"*If* we accept the offer."

"Yes, of course."

Asmat regarded Netoros with another unpleasant look. "So let me see if I understand your offer properly. We invest in Liantac. In exchange, we will receive fifteen per cent of the profits, and we will provide, free of charge, new ferries to bring people here."

Netoros smiled. *She sees providing me with the money to buy out the others as investing in Liantac. Good, good, she understands the realities of the economics.* "Charge whatever you want for the use of the ferries. Since your profit margin is involved, I assume that you would be motivated to improve transportation here. For that matter, your techs might even be able to solve the larik problem."

"How does the Leviathan fit into all this?"

Netoros tilted her head. "It doesn't, exactly. Its occupants, however, do. You see, it is presently full of people that you want."

"That *I* want?"

"Well, that your people want. On that Leviathan are three fugitives from Peacekeeper justice—Dominar Rygel XVI of Hyneria, a Luxan named Ka D'Argo and a Delvian pa'u called Zotoh Zhaan. In addition, there is an alien named John Crichton, who is presently sought after by one of your scientists, Scorpius. If we do consummate our deal, all four of them are yours to do with as you will."

"You have these fugitives in custody?"

"The Leviathan is trapped in orbit. The Hynerian is wearing a collar that prevents him from leaving the Casino. The Delvian is occupied with a fellow member of the Consortium. The Luxan is presently serving as bodyguard for one of my employees. As for Crichton, he's working in one of my offices here on an insoluble problem. They will remain onplanet long enough for us to complete the negotiations." Netoros chuckled. "That, at least, was the plan. I was worried when you did not arrive yesterday. My ability to keep them here legitimately is limited, and I prefer not to antagonize them."

Now Asmat's expression seemed to be questioning Netoros's sanity. "Not to antagonize them?" she repeated. "Why ever not? For that matter, why not just imprison them? You've already got their ship."

"I only have their ship as long as the Clorium field is in place, and I cannot maintain it indefinitely. Besides, as I've said, they've eluded Peacekeeper justice for two cycles. Obviously the direct, antagonistic approach does not work. So I have employed more subtle means. They think they are simply working off a debt, and they will not leave until the debt is paid."

"Very commendable," Asmat said, her voice dripping with sarcasm. "I also want the Leviathan."

"I'm afraid not. I need that to provide transportation. A

Leviathan has much greater passenger capacity than our ferries, not to mention being several orders of magnitude faster. Between that, and providing you lot with the specs for the ferries, we ought to be able to revive Liantac's economy. All I need is your down payment so I can buy out the rest of the Consortium."

"And why is that necessary?"

Netoros frowned. That seemed an odd question for her to ask. "We've gone over all this in our communiqués, Lieutenant."

"Oh, I know the basics—the terms of the deal, the details," Asmat said quickly. "What I want is your *reason* for making this deal. It's all well and good to tell me why *I* should go through with this. However, I'm curious as to why *you* should."

Netoros regarded the Peacekeeper. Asmat returned the look with a hard stare. Her face was a mask—an expression that Peacekeepers were especially skilled at, but one that Asmat had raised to an art form. *She's good, I'll grant her that. I wonder what she could do at a Haunan table . . .*

Her question was a good one, though not one Netoros wanted to answer. It was always best in a negotiation to focus on the person you're negotiating with, not on yourself. *But I can hardly back off from my side of the issue now*, Netoros thought.

Taking a deep breath, she replied, "You're right that our economy is in free fall. Unlike my fellow Consortium members, whose attitude has mostly been to ignore the problem and hope that it goes away, I feel we should *do* something. The Peacekeepers are known throughout the galaxy for being able to . . . do things."

"Yes, but we're generally paid for our services. It seems you're asking us to pay you to help your economy."

"And your own. Oh, I know that the Peacekeepers officially denounce Liantac, but the fact of the matter is, I see plenty of your officers making use of the Casino all the time."

"Really?" Asmat sounded skeptical.

"Don't play the fool with me, Lieutenant. Thori's beak, there are several high-ranking Peacekeepers who have regular seats at my Haunan table. But that's not the point."

"What is the point?" Asmat asked impatiently.

Netoros hesitated. "Do you know what this planet was like before the Casino was built, Lieutenant?"

"No. Nor do I care. I'd just like you to answer my question sometime before I die of old age."

"Bear with me." Netoros stood up. "Hundreds of cycles ago, this world was an arid wasteland."

"This world is *still* an arid wasteland."

Netoros nodded, conceding the point, as she started to pace around the room. "True. But then it was far worse—a place with few natural resources, only a few pitiful attempts at space travel. We weren't even considered worthy of being conquered by any of the great powers of the galaxy. Then, the Casino was built. Suddenly, offworlders became interested in us. By the time I was born, Liantac was a thriving, vibrant planet. Our economy was booming, we were trading with all the major nations—most of which had leaders who had spent at least some time in the Casino—and our economy was strong."

Asmat had not taken her eyes off Netoros.

"Then that frelling idiot blew up a ship, and we've been on a downturn ever since." Netoros walked back to her seat and sat down. "I joined the Consortium in order to make Liantac great again. But the other members don't care about the common good—they just care about lining their own pockets. Their response to the downturn in profits is to raise prices, to increase fines for infractions, to water down the drinks, to rig the gaming tables."

"What's wrong with that?" Asmat asked.

"All that's doing is alienating what little client base we have left. It's only a short-term solution and it doesn't address the overall problem. It's harder for people to come here, and if the Casino becomes known for gouging prices and bad drinks, it'll ruin everything. The Casino's reputation was built on the customers having a good time. Of course, we turned a profit, but enough punters won so that they'd keep coming back. Now, though, fewer punters are winning. It's a bad combination—it's more difficult and more expensive for gamblers to come here for an inferior experience. And it's only going to get worse until we do something about it."

"Or, more to the point, until *you* do something about it," Asmat corrected her.

"Exactly." Netoros walked over to a shelf that contained several electronic readers that were labelled on the side as being financial ledgers. She grabbed one of them. "I took the liberty of compiling some data for you to go over. Financial statements from the Casino, both before and after the catastrophe, and my own projections for profits, should you agree to the terms." She handed Asmat the ledger. "Of course, the profits are based on a percentage of five."

"Then don't bother giving them to me," Asmat said. "I told you before, fifteen percent."

"Ten percent."

Asmat rose and stood nose-to-beak with Netoros. Those narrowed Sebacean eyes were harder than ever. "You seem to be laboring under the delusion that you are negotiating from a position of strength, Netoros. You are not. You need me. I do not need you. If this deal does not go through, nothing changes for the Peacekeepers—except, perhaps, that some of our high-ranking officers won't be able to waste their money at Haunan as easily. So, I repeat—the terms are fifteen percent. That is *not* negotiable."

Netoros knew that Asmat meant to intimidate her. In a sense, she was successful, but perhaps not in the way that Asmat had hoped. Netoros actually was enjoying this immensely. She had spent most of her time fleecing arrogant fools such as the deposed Hynerian, dealing with egotistical imbeciles like Licit, and manipulating the other members of the Consortium. This, though, got her blood boiling, and she had to admit to enjoying sparring with a foe who knew how to fight back.

"I have reserved a room for you at the Esher Hotel,"

Netoros said. "The finest room in my finest hotel. I'll have the figures recalculated for fifteen percent and send then to your room within the arn. In the meantime," she added, selecting a chip from her desk, "this will allow you free access to any part of the Casino owned by me. It also provides you with a stake of a hundred retri, to do with as you will."

Asmat regarded the chip with disdain, but she took it nonetheless. *Of course*, Netoros thought with amusement. *She's still a Peacekeeper. They can make as much noise as they want about their military efficiency, but when you get right down to it, they're mercenaries.*

Heading towards the door, Asmat said, "I will need a solar day to go over the data. We'll speak again at this time tomorrow."

"I look forward to it, Lieutenant."

"Yes," Asmat said as she opened the door. "I'm sure you do."

When the door closed, Netoros sat down at her desk and waved her hand over the intercom. "Celong, please add Lieutenant Asmat to the list for tomorrow's appointments, same time as her arrival today."

"You're scheduled for a meeting with Ornara at that time."

Ornara was a fellow member of the Consortium, and not someone Netoros could easily put off. "Tell Ornara that I'll need to postpone."

"She will not be happy to hear that."

"That, Celong, is her problem. Tell her."

"Of course."

Netoros went back to reading her security report. *Let Ornara be unhappy*, she thought to herself. *Before long, she won't matter.*

"Well, hello there, Commander," said the drunken Sebacean male.

"Lieutenant, actually," Aeryn said, taking a sip of her fifth raslak at the Esher's bar. She had gone to her room upon checking in and composed a message to the others that she would slip to Rygel when they met later. However, that wouldn't be for three-and-a-half arns, so she had decided to kill time at the bar. There was no point in going back up to Moya—Chiana would insist on coming back down to the Casino again if she did, and Aeryn preferred to keep her out of trouble. Neither was there any point in staying in her room and reading over the data Netoros would send, since she was not truly negotiating that deal. And the idea of going to the gambling establishments appealed to her about as much as sex with a Hynerian.

The Sebacean drained his own glass of raslak. "So wha' brings such a lovely lieutenant t' this lovely 'stablishment?"

Without even looking at the drunk, Aeryn replied, "I wanted to have a drink. In solitude."

"Oh, don' be silly. If you wan' solitude, you don' come to a *bar*."

Aeryn found that logic difficult to argue with. "Perhaps not. But I prefer solitude to talking to you."

"Fair 'nough, Major," the Sebacean said with a laugh. "I'll leave you t'your drink." He tried to take another sip, then realized that the glass was empty. "Think I'll have 'nother m'self. Barkeep, another raslak. Make it a double."

"No chance," the bartender said. "You're, whaddayacall, cut off."

"Cut off?" the Sebacean said indignantly. "Wha' for?"

"You've had three raslaks. And I don't know you. Nobody I don't know gets more than three raslaks. You want something nonalcoholic, that's fine. But no more booze."

The Sebacean leaned forward and pointed his finger at the Lian's chest. "Frell you, pal, jus'—jus' frell you."

"Sorry, you're not my type. Now, you want a ker'it tonic or a fruit juice or something, fine." He leaned forward and repeated, "But *no more booze*. Clear?"

"I don' have to put up with this, y'know."

"That's true," the bartender said. "You're free to leave."

"Fine! I think I will!" the Sebacean said, straightening

up and stumbling towards the door. "See 'f I ever come back to *this* place again."

Once the man left, Aeryn turned to the bartender. "You don't know me, either. And this is my fifth raslak. In fact, I'd like a sixth."

"Of course, Lieutenant. Anything you say. And if that man comes back in here to bother you, let me know, and I'll have him dealt with most, whaddayacall, severely."

"That isn't necessary," Aeryn said. "I can take care of myself."

"Of course, of course. I just don't think it's right that a person such as yourself should be harassed by a person such as himself, if you know what I mean."

Aeryn rolled her eyes. "Thank you for your consideration."

"My pleasure, Lieutenant. If there's anything I can do to make your stay more, whaddayacall, comfortable, don't hesitate to ask."

"Two things, actually. Bring me another raslak and leave me the frell alone."

"Of course."

The bartender poured the raslak, placed it in front of Aeryn, and then moved quickly away to serve another customer.

"It's about time," an elderly Lian complained.

"Sorry. Had to get rid of some guy too drunk to realize he was bothering a Peacekeeper."

The Lian straightened. "He must be insane."

"Or suicidal. I got rid of him, though."

"Thank Thori." The Lian shook his head. "Anyhow, get me a frotein."

"Of course."

Sighing, Aeryn drained her raslak in one shot.

It really does make a difference, she thought. She'd been in plenty of places over the last two cycles in civilian garb, and nobody ever treated her any differently than anyone else. *But put me in this uniform, and everyone's sure I'm going to use this pulse rifle if I don't get my way.*

Aeryn looked around. At present, she was sitting near the door at the bar. Nobody had taken the stool to her right or left. In any other bar, those seats would be the first ones occupied.

Aeryn signalled the bartender. "I'm going to a table. Bring me another raslak."

"Right away," the bartender said as he handed the Lian his frotein.

Aeryn was feeling sick. Not just by the bar patrons' behavior, but by her own as well. *I've been out of the Peacekeepers for almost two cycles now. Even if they offered me a full pardon and reinstatement, I wouldn't go back. Yet I was able to slide right back into the old personality without even trying. Netoros bought it, and so does everyone in here.* She looked down. *Is it the uniform? Or is it me?*

The bartender brought Aeryn her raslak. "Here you go. Is everything all right?" he asked.

"Why do you care?" she asked. "Worried that I might shoot up the place?"

"No, Lieutenant, I'm not worried at all. I'll just leave you alone now, if that's what you want."

Damn you, Rygel, for losing Moya and getting me into this, she thought as she finished her drink.

Damn you, Netoros, for sending Rari after us, she thought as she picked up her fresh drink.

Damn you, Stran, for reminding me of the past, she thought as she took a swig of raslak.

And damn you eternally, Crichton, for bringing me to this.

She slammed the empty glass on the table.

Contamination by aliens. If it weren't for you, Crichton, I wouldn't know what a despicable person I was. I wouldn't know the shame and regret. I wouldn't feel anything. I would've just lived my life in ignorance like a good little Peacekeeper and not hated myself so frelling much.

The room started to shimmer and blur. *I think perhaps I've had enough,* Aeryn thought through a raslak-induced haze.

"That's definitely enough," Captain Crais said. "Now you are sure, Officer Sun, that this Technician Stran has been modifying the Fantir Regiment's ships without proper work orders?"

Aeryn stood at attention along with the rest of Icarion Company. They stood in formation before Captain Crais and Lieutenant Teeg. Crais paced back and forth, his hands behind his back. As always, his goatee was neatly trimmed, his hair tied back tightly in its ponytail. Behind him, Teeg was making notes onto a hand-held computer with her usual calm efficiency.

"Very sure, sir," Aeryn said as the captain walked past her. "Stran installed the extra frag cannons on the Fantir Marauder. He says he was simply following orders."

"I'm sure he said that," Crais said drily. "Well, with all these reports confirmed, I'd say we have more than enough to prove their disloyalty. Well done, all of you," he said to all the gathered troops. "I know this was difficult for you. The Fantir Regiment were heroes once—but you have not let sentiment get in the way of your duty, and for that you are all to be commended. Unlike those vile traitors, you have proven yourself today to truly be Peacekeepers."

Aeryn blinked. She hadn't thought about that meeting with Crais in a long time. As she had told Crichton, she'd put it out of her head and moved on to the next duty.

The room blurred again.

Technician Eff Stran was covered in shakan oil. His tech jumpsuit was torn. His short black hair was mussed. He looked disgraceful. "I don't understand what the problem is, Officer Sun," he said. "I was simply doing my duty."

"Doing your duty requires checking work orders, Technician. It also requires maintaining your appearance."

"Officer Sun, I've been working constantly for the last thirty arns—we're short-handed and we've had to refit four ships that took heavy damage against the Scarren. I've barely eaten or slept in two solar days. It's been like this pretty regularly lately. So no, I probably haven't checked every single work order that came in. If High Command *would actually send replacements when we request them, then perhaps I—"*

Aeryn lost patience. *"I don't have time to listen to your feeble excuses, Technician! You can rest assured that your actions will be reported."*

Stran's face went ashen. *"What actions? Officer, I was just following orders. Since when is that a crime?"*

Disgusted with this pathetic tech, Aeryn left the maintenance bay without another word. She had little respect for techs—they thought themselves so essential, but mostly they were a bunch of excuse-making pewnkahs.

The sooner this one was imprisoned, the better.

Again, Aeryn blinked. She started to sip her raslak, then thought better of it.

Velorek was being held by two other commandos, weak and broken. He looked at her, pleading, desperate for her to acknowledge his existence. But even though Aeryn had shared her bed with him, she now felt nothing but contempt. He was, after all, an alien sympathizer who had tried to sabotage Captain Crais's Leviathan project. He deserved whatever he got.

That was why Aeryn had turned him in.

He tried to reason with her, but she had cut him off and spat in his face.

"You are nothing to me."

"Nothing to me."

"Well done, all of you."

"I don't have time to listen to your feeble excuses, Technician!"

"I was just following orders. Since when is that a crime?"

"You have proven yourselves today to truly be Peacekeepers."

"What brings a beautiful Sebacean like you to a place like this?"

Aeryn blinked once more. "What?"

It was Rygel. *It must be midday*, she thought. She wondered how many raslaks she'd drunk since she lost count.

"A creature as attractive as you shouldn't be drinking alone, my dear. May I join you?"

Aeryn sneered while palming the message chip in her belt. "Get 'way from me, you Hynerian trog," she said with a sneer as she slipped the chip under the cushion of Rygel's ThroneSled.

Rygel grabbed her hand. It felt even clammier than usual to her. He surreptitiously handed her a chip of his own. "Very well, Peacekeeper. Rest assured, you *will* regret rebuffing me."

"Regret rebuffing some idiot Hynerian with a debtor's collar? Don' make me *laugh*."

Pulling himself up to his full height—a sad sight for a sitting Hynerian—Rygel retorted, "Good day," and left the bar.

Aeryn waited a few microts, pocketed the chip, got up, and went to the bar. "What do I owe you?" she said, trying to enunciate and only partially succeeding.

As obsequious as ever, the bartender replied, "Oh, it's on the house, Lieutenant."

I have proven myself today to truly be a Peacekeeper.

Aeryn spat on the bartender the same way she had spat on Velorek after she'd turned him in. The same way she'd wanted to spit on Stran when she'd turned him in.

"You make me sick," she said. Then she looked at the rest of the bar's patrons. "You *all* make me sick!"

Dozens of frightened eyes stared at her—Lian, Sebacean, Halosian, Delvian. Many gazes darted to her rifle. She was tempted to raise it.

Instead, she went back to her room.

If only there was some way I could spit on myself.

CHAPTER 10

Rygel read over the contents of the chip that Aeryn had provided. It didn't surprise him that Netoros had a greater plan in mind than simply fleecing Moya's crew. The plan was too elaborate to have such a minimal payoff. In Rygel's experience, people like Netoros didn't go to the kind of trouble she had gone through with Rari to track Moya down unless she had something really big planned. The tasks they had been assigned—bodyguarding and busywork—were not sufficient to the magnitude of the lure.

What Aeryn had learned, however, most certainly was.

The question now is, what is to be done about it?

Rygel hated asking such complex questions on empty stomachs. Unfortunately, he had no money to purchase food.

So we'll have to rectify that, won't we?

A quick check of a directory revealed a large gambling establishment called Ornara's Emporium. An equally quick inquiry revealed that Ornara was, in fact, another member of the Consortium. While it was true that Rygel had already made nice with Garess, that was not a stable thing—particularly after Garess made his inevitable move on Zhaan.

It's better to have more allies than fewer—and it definitely behooves me to befriend another member of the Consortium. After all, Netoros plans to buy them all out, so they're her enemies whether they realize it or not. And I'm just the one to call it to their attention.

Crichton had a saying—and unlike the other inane maxims he spouted, this one actually made sense: "The enemy of my enemy is my friend."

Rygel entered Ornara's Emporium and was immediately greeted by a tall, wiry Lian with dark blue feathers. "May I help you, sir?"

"Yes, you may. Point me to your Haunan table. And I will, of course, expect a line of credit."

The Lian had started to walk towards the interior of the establishment, but then stopped. "In that case, sir, I'm afraid we're going to require some—collateral."

Rygel's ears shot upward. "I beg your pardon?"

"I'm sorry, sir, but—"

"Do you have any idea who I am?"

"Yes, sir. You are Dominar Rygel XVI of Hyneria. We are, of course, honored by your presence, but unfortunately, we do have a policy regarding anyone wearing one of those collars, sir. We are already aware of the fact that you are unable to offer your vessel as collateral, as the ship is part of the debt represented by the collar."

Maneuvering his ThroneSled closer to the Lian, Rygel said in a low voice, "First of all, my servants are presently working off the debt so that my ship will be available."

"But it is not available now, sir, and—"

"Secondly," Rygel said, ignoring the interruption, "the ship and the contents of the ship are not the same thing. I have quite a bit of—collateral aboard Moya that is *still* mine."

"If not for that collar, sir, I would be happy to take your word for it, but I'm afraid I must verify this. We will need to contact your ship."

Only Chiana's aboard, Rygel thought. This was promising. Of all the crew, she was the one most likely to support his desire to gamble. *Good thing D'Argo isn't up there.*

"Very well," he said haughtily.

He led Rygel to a back section of the place, which held a communications array. Within microts, the Lian had opened a channel to Pilot. "I wish to speak to someone in authority on your ship, please."

"I will connect you with Chiana," Pilot said. Rygel wondered if he detected a note of irony in Pilot's voice.

After several more microts: *"This is Chiana. What do you want?"*

"My name is Rolin, madam, from Ornara's Emporium. I'm performing a routine credit check on Dominar Rygel XVI. I need to verify that he has at least a hundred retri worth of collateral in his possession on board your ship."

"Oh, really?"

Rygel's moustache flared. *Curse you, you Nebari trill, if you ruin this for me, I'll . . .*

"Well, let me assure you, Rolin, that Dominar Rygel XVI, does not have a hundred retri worth of collateral . . ."

"I see," Rolin said, gravely.

Rygel was on the verge of exploding.

"It's more like a thousand. Extend him all the credit you want."

"Ah." Rolin looked relieved. "Thank you so much, madam. Sorry to have disturbed you."

"Not at all. Happy to be of help."

"Fa-pu-ta," Rygel muttered as his intestinal tract settled down.

Rolin pulled a chip from his jacket, punched some buttons on it, then handed it to Rygel. "You now have five hundred retri in credit. Welcome to the Emporium, and please feel free to partake of our complimentary buffet."

"Thank you, I will," Rygel said graciously. He was willing to overlook the man's behavior given the end result. Besides, Rolin was simply doing his job.

Rygel gambled better on full stomachs—in fact, he generally did everything better on full stomachs—so he stuffed himself at the buffet before finally settling down at the Haunan table.

The others would have fits if they saw me now, the yotzes, he thought. They didn't understand, of course, but Rygel had grown accustomed to that. The crew was constantly underestimating him. The only reason he'd lost before was because Netoros had cheated—and, as they'd learned, Netoros had good reason to cheat him. Under normal circumstances, there was no point in the owner cheating a player at Haunan. The house always took a small percentage of every pot no matter who won, and Netoros had accrued a respectable amount in the game she and Rygel had been involved in.

Rygel took a seat at a Haunan table that had just lost a player. Three Lians sat at the table. "Greetings," he said. "I take it the usual rules apply?"

"Naturally," the dealer said.

"Excellent." He plugged his chip in, and the readout showed his five hundred retri. "Let the game commence." He flagged down one of the staff. "Fetch me some marjools, will you?"

"Of course, sir," the Lian waiter replied.

Rygel put in his ante, and the dealer laid out the first hand. The Hynerian found himself with two paladins. *Frelling wonderful,* he thought, and folded.

The next three hands were similar, and Rygel found his credit dwindling. *This is not good. My possessions on Moya—at least the ones I'm actually willing to part with— are worth considerably less than five hundred retri. Perhaps Chiana should have been a trifle more restrained in vouching for me.*

He put in his ante for the fifth hand, and got a king up— and another king down. *This is more like it.*

The down cards were all kings, with his other two up cards being paladins. Conveniently, one of the other players had two queens showing, and was raising the bets with great enthusiasm. Rygel let him build the pot. *Given the*

*way he's betting, he's either got two queens in the hole, or
he's trying to bluff everyone out of the game.*

If it was the latter strategy, it worked on the other two.
They dropped out quickly. Rygel, however, stayed in, never
raising. Best of all, it didn't matter to Rygel—even if his
opponent had all four queens, Rygel's four kings would
win.

Finally, the pot reached four hundred and fifty retri, of
which a hundred and forty was Rygel's.

"All bets have been matched," the dealer announced.
"Players, show your hands."

The Lian sat up straighter. "Four queens," he said.

A murmur of approval went around the table.

Slowly, deliberately, Rygel turned over each king without saying a word.

The Lian slumped in his seat. "Thori's beak," he muttered.

Rygel simply smiled as the number on the display in
front of him increased by four hundred and thirty. The
house, after all, had to have its cut.

"I'd like to thank you once again for allowing me to tour
the arboretum, and for letting me to take this lovely
dav'mak flower," Zhaan said to Arco as the servant led her
through the large door. "Are you sure Garess won't mind?"
she asked, stroking the lustrous black-and-white-striped
ovoid petals.

"I will confess, Pa'u," Arco said, "that I did not obtain
permission. However, there are many dav'mak flowers in
the arboretum so I am sure this one will not be missed."

Arco coded the lock before leading Zhaan towards the
workshop

Zhaan smiled at the servant. *I expect you'll feel differently if I am forced to use this flower the way I suspect I
shall have to.* Aloud, she asked, "Has Dominar Rygel returned?"

Arco shot her a look of dismay. "I was not aware that
he was coming back."

"I am expecting him, yes," Zhaan said, and her smile widened. It was clear that Arco was not looking forward to Rygel's reappearance.

"If you will excuse me, madam, I'm afraid I must hasten to the kitchen. The cook was planning a celebration in honor of the dominar's departure. I must break the sad news to her and give her the opportunity to prepare for his arrival."

Bowing her head slightly, Zhaan said, "Of course."

Nice to see that Rygel's appetite will be someone else's problem for a change. Still, she wondered where the Hynerian had gone. He was supposed to meet up with Aeryn at that hotel bar, then come back. Aeryn was providing information on her meeting with Netoros, which would determine what action she and the others took.

Goddess willing, Rygel won't get into any more trouble, she thought, then realized that the oath was wasted. *Of course he will get into more trouble. He is Rygel.*

Deciding that she would deal with it if and when she had to, Zhaan put thoughts of Rygel out of her mind and returned to the workshop.

Her own course of action would likely remain unchanged: continue to work on the plants until Garess made a move to imprison her—if, indeed, their theory about the extra display case was correct. Zhaan, however, felt quite sure that it was and that Garess would eventually tip his hand.

She had no intention of allowing him to succeed. Once, she had been imprisoned by a botanist named Br'Nee, who had intended to keep Zhaan as a sample. Br'Nee had miniaturized her and placed her in a test tube for scientific purposes; Garess apparently intended to place her in stasis in an open display case in order to show her off as a part of his collection. She had fought hard and risked much for her freedom from the Peacekeepers, but even they had allowed her the ability to move and think within her cell—enough so that she could overcome the rage within her and become a pa'u. She swore by the Goddess that she would not allow herself to be imprisoned again.

She sat down at the table. Of the fourteen samples, Zhaan had identified twelve, though she'd only recorded eleven. She could easily have completed the other two by now, but she was still stalling. She had delayed things by asking for a tour of the arboretum, which took a good two arns, but there were limits to how much she could slow down her work.

Now she focused on her defense against Garess's likely attack. She'd been concerned as to how she would respond to any attempt by the Lian to entrap her, but the dav'mak flower would provide the answer. Violence was an absolute last resort. It was dangerous to allow the murderous rage within her to come to the fore. *It will take more than a fool of a collector to bring me to that point again*, she thought.

Within microts, she was back at the table, pretending to struggle over the identity of the stems that she was certain were siwains. Instead she was slicing off the petals of the dav'mak and mixing it with the remains of one of the siwain samples that she had pulverized.

By the time Zhaan had finished the mixture. Rygel still had not come back. She tapped her comm. "Rygel, come in, this is Zhaan."

There was no reply.

"Rygel, where are you?"

Still silence.

Zhaan pretended to examine the siwain while wondering what Rygel was doing.

Soon, Garess came in with another Lian, whom Zhaan did not recognize. The newcomer had speckled brown feathers and hooded eyes. Zhaan took an immediate dislike to him.

"Can I help you?" she asked, sparing them only a quick glance.

"Actually, I'd say that the help you can provide has come to an end," said Garess. "I have managed to confirm the final three plants from an independent source. In case you were wondering, they are a siwain, a lipchik and a Luxan hawkbud."

Zhaan was surprised. "Are you sure about the hawkbud?"

"Quite sure. We're ready to put all the new samples in their display cases."

"Excellent," Zhaan said, standing up. "Then my task is complete, and my portion of the debt to Netoros is paid." *Now is when we shall learn whether or not Rygel's theory was correct.*

A part of Zhaan—the part that had dedicated her life to the Delvian Seek, the part that wanted to believe in the inherent good in people—hoped that this was all a misunderstanding. That part hoped that she and Rygel were wrong about Garess's motives and that he was going to let her go on her merry way.

That part of Zhaan was often disappointed, and this occasion was no different. The Lian standing next to Garess raised a weapon.

"I'm afraid not," Garess said politely. "You see, I am a collector. It is vital that I have *every* known plant in my arboretum—otherwise the collection is not complete. The one thing that was vexing me, however, was the lack of a Delvian."

Garess began to pace about the room. The brown-feathered Lian kept his weapon trained on Zhaan. She did not move, though she had gathered some of the dav'mak-and-siwain mixture in her hand.

"It's difficult, of course. There are very few sentient plants in the galaxy, and most of them are relatively easy to obtain. You may have noticed the three krem'ts in the back of the arboretum. The krem't are sentient, but as long as you provide them with water and light, and allow them to debate higher philosophy and sing periodically, they don't care what you do with them. But you Delvians are a tricky bunch. You don't grow roots. Instead, you're bipedal. It's a biological peculiarity. I've always found you Delvians terribly fascinating."

Garess was now fairly close to Zhaan. *This won't do*, she thought. *I need him to be standing near the other one if this is to work.*

"But it also makes keeping one of you captive a problem. However, I was pleased to finally have a solution to that quandary when I acquired the stasis units that could be attached to the case material. Then all I needed was a Delvian." He regarded Zhaan with that twinkle. "So generous of Netoros to provide me with one."

"I do not believe that Netoros will be happy with your taking me prisoner," Zhaan said.

"Your opinion of yourself is high, Pa'u. You imagine that Netoros will perhaps take umbrage—demand some action be taken in your defense?" He laughed. "I'm afraid not. Netoros is a junior member of the Consortium and in no position to take *any* action against me. Besides, I seriously doubt she cares that much, as long as she gets some kind of restitution from me in exchange for providing me with your assistance—which, you can be sure, she will." Garess walked back towards the other Lian. "I would like to thank you once again, Pa'u. You have been invaluable to me."

"I would say you're welcome, but that would be a lie," Zhaan said calmly. "However, you would be mistaken to assume that I need someone else to take action in my defense. Perhaps you are not aware of my connection with Rygel. You see, he and I were both prisoners of the Peacekeepers."

Garess's eyes widened. The other Lian didn't flinch or blink, but kept his weapon steadily on Zhaan. *Quite the professional*, Zhaan thought.

She continued. "I was imprisoned on the charge of murder. Specifically, the murder of my lover."

"But you're a *priest*," Garess said.

"Now I am, yes. That is why I will not kill you." Then, in a quick motion she raised her right hand to her mouth and blew, being careful not to inhale any of the mixture herself. The effect was instantaneous—both Garess and the other Lian inhaled the mixture and were immediately paralyzed. "Instead, I have chosen a more benign method of defending myself. You have been stopped by a mixture that comes from your own plant samples, Garess. Ironic, isn't it?"

Garess could only gurgle.

"How long you remain paralyzed varies from species to species. However, I have never known it to last less than fourteen arns."

Another gurgling sound.

"It could, of course, be longer, since I have never used it on a Lian. I will take my leave of you now. Perhaps you will not be so cavalier with other lives in the future." She smiled sweetly. "But I doubt it, somehow. Goodbye, Garess."

Zhaan strode confidently out of the room.

It was only after Rygel's winnings had grown to fifteen hundred retri—actually a thousand, counting the five hundred in credit—that Rolin, the tall, blue-feathered Lian that he had met earlier, walked up to him and whispered in his ear. "Sir, Ornara, the owner of the establishment, would like to invite you to dine with her."

Rygel had no idea how much time had passed since his arrival. Like any good gambling establishment, Ornara's Emporium kept no timepieces on display—one way management encouraged people to lose track of time. But he knew it had been quite a while since he'd eaten.

He touched a button that put a hold on his winnings, then entered the password that would protect it. "I shall be happy to dine with Ornara. Deal me out."

Rolin led him through the back toward the restaurant that was attached to the game room. The moment he crossed the threshold, Rygel's comm sounded with Zhaan's voice. *"Rygel, come in please!"*

Rygel's ears drooped. Zhaan had probably been trying to get in touch with him for some time, but the game room walls no doubt contained some kind of dampening agent that prevented unauthorized communications from going in and out. *After all, you don't want the gamblers distracted by outside calls.*

"Excuse me, Rolin," Rygel said. "One of my servants is calling."

Maneuvering his ThroneSled to a corner, Rygel whispered, "What do you want, Zhaan?"

"As your 'servant', sweet Rygel, I think I'm entitled to know where you are. You were supposed to have come back here immediately after meeting with Aeryn."

"I'm busy right now, Zhaan. Call back later."

"Rygel, I just left Garess—he tried to imprison me."

"I take it he failed," Rygel said drily.

"Obviously."

"You didn't kill him, did you?"

"What do you think?"

"I think you're trying to frighten me. Kindly don't. The last thing we need right now is to have the death of a Consortium member on our hands."

"Says the Hynerian who lost Moya in a card game."

"I was cheated!"

"So you say."

"Look, according to Aeryn, Netoros has negotiated a major deal with the Peacekeepers that includes turning us over to them. She contrived all of this to keep us here for the Peacekeepers."

"Really? How nice of you to share that information, Rygel. If you had returned to Garess's as you were supposed to, I'd already know that."

"As if I am some errand boy. I am Dominar—"

"—Rygel XVI and you'll go where you please. Yes, I know. I could hardly forget, what with your constant reminders."

"Look, Zhaan," Rygel said, trying to keep his voice down, "I've been invited to dine with Ornara, another member of the Consortium. We need someone like her on our side. Unless you think Garess will be amenable to helping us out after whatever you did to him."

"Probably not."

"As I suspected. Now go away and leave me in peace!"
With that, Rygel cut the connection.

Time to get to work.

Rolin led Rygel into the restaurant. The dominar was
pleased to see how well appointed it was. This was no
simple eatery, but a place where the wealthiest patrons—
the high rollers—had their meals. The tables were all made
of what appeared to be natural wood—a rarity on this
planet—and the plush chairs looked to Rygel's practiced
eye to be made from the finest animal skins.

Rygel looked at the plates of the various customers he
passed as Rolin led him to the rear section—they were all
laden with large portions, and the drinks were in generous-
sized bowls. *Good, good*, Rygel thought. *If I'm going to be
treated to a meal, it should be the finest.*

They arrived at a large corner table. A plump female with
short white feathers and black, beady eyes was already
seated there. To Rygel's surprise, she already had plenty of
food in front of her. *I would have thought*, he thought huff-
ily, *that she would wait for her guest to arrive before or-
dering.*

"Dominar Rygel XVI," Rolin said, "this is Ornara."

"Ah, excellent, excellent!" Ornara said. Her voice thun-
dered throughout the restaurant, but she did not get up. "A
pleasure to make your acquaintance, Dominar. Please, have
a seat!"

By the Hynerian gods, Rygel thought, as he positioned
his ThroneSled opposite Ornara, *she makes D'Argo sound
timid.*

"The pleasure is mine, Ornara. I seem to have had the
good fortune of meeting several members of your esteemed
Consortium."

Ornara leaned forward and pecked a piece of meat out of
her bowl. It appeared to be some kind of game animal that
Rygel didn't recognize, though it looked and smelled especially tasty. Ornara swallowed it before replying. "Really? I
know that you met Netoros, of course. The unfortunate story

of your little Haunan game has spread, I'm afraid. Plus, of course, you're wearing her collar."

Rygel sighed. He'd actually managed to forget that the collar was there, but as soon as Ornara mentioned it, the damned thing started to itch again.

"Bring the dominar whatever he wants," Ornara instructed the waiter she had beckoned.

"In that case," Rygel said with a smile, "a platter of marjools with Tulan relish, some limmok, a plate of Hepatian minced stew, some Cholian curd salad, a bowl of huulo fruit in cream, and a flagon of your finest wine. Oh, and whatever it is that Ornara's having."

The waiter's eyes had widened as Rygel's order had continued. "Will there be anything else?"

"Perhaps later on, but that will do for now."

Ornara laughed heartily. "I like your style, Dominar."

"Funny, Garess said much the same thing."

Ornara's eyes got beadier at the mention of her fellow Consortium member. "You've met Garess?"

Play this hand carefully, Dominar, Rygel thought. *See what her relationship is with Garess before revealing your hole card.* "Yes. As a favor to Netoros, one of my servants has been identifying some of his plants. Part of my agreement with Netoros for removing this collar," he added sourly.

"That's odd," Ornara said, looking perplexed.

"What's odd?" Rygel demanded, digging in to his curd salad.

"It's odd that Garess needs someone to identify those ridiculous plants of his and that Netoros would try to curry favor with him."

Nodding and swallowing more salad, Rygel said, "Ah, I see."

"I doubt that, Dominar—and that is to your benefit. Believe me, the last thing you want to do is get involved in our politics!" Ornara said with a hearty laugh.

"Don't be so sure about that. After all, I *am* a politician."

After a thoughtful pause, Ornara bent down to peck at

her meal. "Let us simply say that the Consortium would be better off with fewer eccentric old fools like Garess and fewer naive young fools like Netoros."

Rygel gulped some wine. "Of all the words I'd use to describe Netoros, 'naive' is not one that springs to mind."

"Oh, she has a good enough business sense. And she knows how to win at Haunan," Ornara said with a sly look. "But her ideas are a bit too—radical. Unfortunately, if she ties herself too closely to Garess, it could be disastrous. He's fairly influential—or could be, if he put his mind to it. But, this obsession with his arboretum . . ." Ornara's voice trailed off. "Personally," she continued with a laugh, "I prefer to eat my plants!" As if to emphasize the point, she pecked at the leaves that garnished her meat.

Polishing off his salad, Rygel said, "I quite agree."

"But enough about that. I can't imagine you truly find this interesting. You're just letting an old Lian babble on because she's buying you lunch. I'm much more interested in you."

Actually, for once, I'm more interested in the babblings of an old Lian, Rygel thought. However, he was sure he could get the conversation back on track by the time his huulo fruit arrived.

Ornara lapped up some of her drink, then said, "I'm told that you've been doing phenomenally well at the Haunan table. And that you were also doing quite well before Netoros forced that collar on you."

"I miscalculated," Rygel said tightly, not wishing to dwell on this subject. The waiter brought the marjools. Rygel grabbed a handful and stuffed them in his mouth.

"Oh, I doubt that very much. You see, I have the Haunan tables watched very closely. My analysts keep constant reports on who's winning and losing, and what their style of play is." Ornara's voice had become surprisingly subdued. Now she was speaking so quietly that Rygel could barely hear her. "Would you like to know what they said about you?"

No gambler liked to have his methods analyzed, but Rygel had to admit to being curious in this case. "Yes, I would."

"You were described, Dominar, as one of the smartest players to come into the emporium in cycles. That you never stay in the game unless you intend to win. That, in fact, you won every hand you stayed in on until the end with only a few exceptions, and those exceptions fell within the realm of bad luck, or situations where it would have been impossible for you to predict the winner's hand."

Rygel knew where this was going, but pretended not to. "What is your point, Ornara?"

"My point, Dominar, is that there's no way you could possibly have lost that hand to Netoros. She had three kings showing. You would not have remained in so long with four queens unless you were *absolutely* sure that she did not have the fourth king."

Rygel smiled. If only his shipmates understood Haunan as well as Ornara did. *So nice to talk to someone who speaks the same language, as it were.* "I see your analysts aren't limited to your own game."

Back in the bellowing tone and accompanied by the hearty laugh, Ornara replied, "All good owners keep an eye on the competition, and we of the Consortium are, by definition, good owners!"

"To answer the question you seem unwilling to ask," Rygel said, swallowing the last of his marjools just as the waiter brought the stew, "yes, I do believe that Netoros cheated me. Unfortunately, I have no proof, so it would be my word against hers. Much as I would like to think that the word of a dominar can be trusted without question, the reality is that I would not be believed. A sad commentary on the state of affairs in the universe today, but there it is."

Another hearty laugh. "Come now, Dominar, you of all people should appreciate that, when it comes to Haunan, there are no dominars, no Consortium members—simply winners and losers! And you came up a loser! Now why is that?"

"I've already told you—because I was cheated," Rygel said, shovelling some stew into his mouth with the spoon that the waiter had provided.

Ornara waved her hand. "No, no, you misunderstand—*why* were you cheated? There was no need! After all, with a pot that large, Netoros stood to make a tidy profit just on her percentage. No, she had to have another reason for cheating you. And I'm very interested in knowing what that reason is."

Rygel smiled. *That was the cue I've been waiting for.* He took a sip of his wine. "Well, let's discuss that, shall we?"

CHAPTER 11

*J*ohn, where are you?"

Aeryn's voice on his comm started Crichton out of his reverie. It was all well and good to pretend to be working on the larik particles problem even though he had, in fact, already solved it. Now he was back to trying to reconstruct the lyrics to "Viva Las Vegas," but he still couldn't get past the first line. *Face it, John-boy, the only way you're gonna get the lyrics to the song is if you bump into Elvis his own self.*

Aloud he said to Aeryn, "Same place I've been for the last solar day. Why?"

"I need t'talk t'you right away. Can y'meet me?"

"I don't think it'd be such a hot idea for me to leave here. I'm supposed to be working for the greater good of Liantac, remember?"

Aeryn let out a surprisingly loud snort. *"I wouldn' worry 'bout that."*

"You okay, Aeryn?"

"I'm jus' fine, why?"

"You're drunk, aren't you?" Crichton could hardly believe it.

"Tha's ridic'lous."

"So how come you can't pronounce 'ridiculous'?"

"Look, will you jus' meet me? I don' wanna talk over the comm."

"All right, fine, I'll meet you. Hell, you toasted is a sight I'd pay money to see. I'll just tell Netoros I need a break. Where are you?"

"Esher Hotel. Room 1969."

"Fine. I'll be right there."

"See ya."

Crichton was concerned. *Aeryn drunk. This can't be good,* he thought. *If she felt the need to tie one on, she's probably in worse shape than she's willing to admit.* He chuckled bitterly. *Right, like she's ever willing to admit when she's in bad shape. But between that Stran dude and having to play PK again, she's probably a big ol' mess.*

The question, as always, was whether or not Aeryn would actually let Crichton help her or if she'd push him away. Again.

He transferred all his work to a chip, then wiped it all from the computer. *Wouldn't want Netoros to get her grubby hands on my notes—at least not before I'm ready for her.*

He'd have to pass Celong's desk on the way out. Netoros's assistant looked totally absorbed in her work.

"I'm takin' a break," he said.

"I beg your pardon?"

Who is she anyway, my fourth-grade teacher? "A break. A pause. A time-out. A lull in the action."

"I'm familiar with the meaning of the word, however—"

"I've been starin' at that computer so long my eyeballs are gonna fall out. I need a break. So I'm taking it. I don't see the problem here."

"Very well. But try to be back soon. The work you are doing is very important."

"So they keep telling me." He flashed her a peace sign and said, "Later."

"And if you should find that your eyeballs do fall out, Netoros will, I'm sure, cover all your medical needs," Celong called after him.

Crichton whirled around, but Celong was already back at work. *Maybe she actually has a sense of humor*, Crichton thought to himself.

He took the speedy lift down, grateful that he hadn't eaten recently, then headed to the Esher.

Part of him was sorry that he couldn't go to the roof of Netoros's office complex and declare his triumph to the heavens. *Of course, the Casino's in a dome, so the heavens probably wouldn't hear, but still . . .* He had solved the problem of the larik particles. It would still require a practical test to be absolutely sure, but every sim he'd run indicated that it would work.

What was especially gratifying was that only he could have come up with it. Over time, he had been forced to incorporate some of Moya's bio-mechanical components into his *Farscape I* module. After all, proper replacement parts were pretty much impossible to come by. Besides, he had enjoyed the challenge of melding the two technologies together, and it served to make the module a better ship.

Of course, everyone from Aeryn and D'Argo to that mechanic Furlow at Dam-Ba-Da Depot had all tried repeatedly to convince him that no improvements could help and that he should just junk *Farscape I*.

That ain't never gonna happen. And it's a good thing, too, 'cause without my module, this planet would still be in deep dren.

Several of *Farscape I*'s systems were completely incompatible with anything on this end of the universe. The technologies simply hadn't developed in the same direction, and there was no way to reconcile them. One such system was the exhaust. Crichton had once spent a good week going over the exhaust systems of both *Farscape I* and Aeryn's Prowler, comparing and contrasting them, and finding that they had more or less nothing in common aside from over-all function. *Like watching a DVD on your computer versus watching the same thing broadcast on TV—two completely different technologies but the same basic result.*

One of those differences meant that a simple adjustment to the intake valves would allow *Farscape I* to keep the larik particles out. That same adjustment was impossible to make on any of the intakes that were used in this neck of the galaxy—indeed, such adjustments were the first thing that was attempted thirty cycles ago. *So much for Mr. Back-wards Technology. I* am *the man. John Robert Crichton Jr., Ph.D. and all-around brilliant dude, has saved the day.*

On the way to the Esher, more chips were pressed into Crichton's hands, allowing him ingress to the finest spots on the greatest planet in the galaxy. *I should probably hang onto these suckers and sell them in bulk on the next com-merce planet*, he mused.

He shook his head and smiled as he entered the hotel. *Damn. I* have *been hanging around Rygel and Chiana too long . . .*

The Esher's lift managed the impressive feat of being worse than the one in Netoros's complex, and Crichton fell more than stepped out at the nineteenth floor. *I am definitely going to sic the Otis people on whoever designed these damn elevators.*

The door to Aeryn's room was open.

The place was *huge*. Aeryn was sitting at the foot of a bed large enough to sleep four.

"How'd you rate *this* place? I've been in smaller aircraft hangars."

"It's jus' another frelling extravagance," Aeryn said with as venomous a tone as Crichton had ever heard her use. "Everything here is done t'excess, or hadn't you noticed?"

Aeryn was pale and sweating. Her eyes were bloodshot, and her hair was tangled.

"Damn, Aeryn, you *are* drunk."

"I'm *not* drunk."

"Aeryn, you are baked, boiled, bombed, toasted, tipsy,

chicken fried, and wasted. You're as drunk as a skunk," Crichton drawled, using two syllables to pronounce "drunk."

"Jus' a few drinks before I met Rygel."

"Aeryn, I can smell the raslak from here. If I lit a match, your breath would ignite it."

"Look, we need t'talk, so if you're finished assassinating my character, can we get on with it, please?"

"I'm not assassinating anything, Aeryn," Crichton said, walking closer to her. "I'm just trying to get you to admit that you're drunk. I'm trying to get Officer Aeryn Sun, winner of the Pickle-Up-Her-Butt Award for six cycles running, to admit that she's swizzled."

Aeryn stood up, slamming her hand down on the bed as she did so. "I am *not* drunk! I—"

Suddenly, her skin tone went from pale to a rather unfortunate shade of green. "Frell . . ." she said in a very small voice, and ran into the bathroom.

Crichton waited until the sounds of her retching ended. He wanted to go in to check on her, but figured that would be tantamount to suicide. Instead, he looked intently at the hideous painting that hung over the bed. It portrayed a vaguely pastoral setting, with a small representation of a Lian lying down under a scraggly tree.

When a pale-faced Aeryn came out of the bathroom, Crichton said, "Somehow it just figures. I travel halfway across the galaxy where everything is different—but even here, they manage to find the ugliest damn paintings to put in hotel rooms."

"Never mind your frelling homeworld," she said, "we need to talk."

"Hey, don't knock Earth, Aeryn—if it weren't for my homeworld and its incredibly brilliant method of designing exhaust systems, I wouldn't have the solution to all this world's problems."

"That's what I want to talk to you about," Aeryn said, slowly moving to one of the large chairs and sitting down. "The work you've done on solving the larik problem. I assume you have it and didn't do anything stupid like leaving it on Netoros's computer?"

"Your confidence is greatly appreciated," Crichton said with an annoyed glare. "Of course I did."

"You left it on the computer?" Aeryn said with a gasp.

"No!" *Sweet Mother McCree, she really is drunk.* "I meant, of course I brought it with me."

"Good. You need to destroy the chip."

"Okay, the translator microbes must be on the fritz," Crichton said, "because I'd swear you just said I should destroy the chip."

"Yes, I did, and I meant it. Anything that makes this place accessible to the Peacekeepers should be avoided."

Crichton took Aeryn's former seat at the foot of the bed. "Aeryn, the Peacekeepers aren't going to come here, remember? You're the Peacekeepers, as far as Netoros is concerned."

Aeryn attempted a smile. "Not as far as the Peacekeepers are concerned. They thought enough of this deal to send a lieutenant here. When she doesn't report back, they will investigate."

"What's your point, Aeryn?"

Letting out a long breath, she said, "This place used to be off-limits to the Peacekeepers. Now they're in negotiations with Netoros to take over the world."

That got Crichton's attention. "Take over?"

"Yes." Aeryn then proceeded to give the details of her conversation with Netoros.

Crichton stood back up and started to pace. "Suddenly, it all makes sense. The PKs finance her takeover of the Consortium, they get a nice steady stream of winnings to finance their ongoing attempt to be the biggest badasses in the galaxy."

"Crichton, will you please stop pacing?" Aeryn pleaded. "You're giving me a headache."

"Sorry," Crichton said, and sat back down on the bed.

"The point is, this is just part of a larger picture. The Peacekeepers have been making more and more inroads into the Uncharted Territories lately. They gave Crais permission to search for us here, Scorpius built his Gammak base here, there was Larraq's mission—and now this."

Not to mention PK infiltration of the Royal Planet, Crichton thought, remembering Jena, who had been assigned to make sure the Scarrens didn't get a toehold amongst the Sebacean expatriates on that world. Crichton hadn't told the others about her—that was the price he'd had to pay for her not killing him—so Aeryn didn't know about that. *But it supports her argument.*

"All right, fine, the PKs are movin' on up to the east side. What does that have to do with my work on the larik problem?"

"The best reason that the Peacekeepers would have to invest in this planet is if it is returned to its former glory. The best reason that they wouldn't is if the place is only accessible by a decaying ferry system. You have to eliminate your work. Netoros wasn't even expecting you to be able to find a solution, so it's not like anyone will be surprised at the lack of results."

Crichton shook his head. "No."

Aeryn blinked. "Now *my* microbes must be on the friss. Did you say no?"

"It's 'on the fritz', and yeah, I said no. And I meant no."

"Crichton—"

Holding up a hand, Crichton said, "I know what you're gonna say, Aeryn." In what he thought was a passable imitation of Aeryn, he continued, "'You didn't listen to me when I said not to come to this frelling planet and look what happened?' And you're right, coming here probably was a mistake. But you said Netoros was the only one who wanted to deal with the Peacekeepers. If anybody else wanted in, she'd be partnered up with them, but it's a solo deal for her, right?"

"Yes."

"Then there's no need to destroy the work. We just don't give it to her."

"Crichton, it's safer if we don't give it to *anyone*."

Closing his eyes and sighing, Crichton said, "You don't get it, do you?" He shook his head. "Don't answer that—of course you don't get it. You're a commando, not a tech. I was hoping that when you saved Rygel that time it mighta rubbed off, but it obviously didn't."

"What're you blathering about now, Crichton?" Aeryn had the frelling-idiot look on her face again.

"Aeryn, for two cycles I've been cut off from everything. My home, my family, my friends, my language—I'm not even thinking in years and seconds anymore, it's 'cycles' and 'microts'. Hell, I can't even remember the words to one of my favorite songs. I've nearly died more than once. I've had my brain turned inside out. I've produced a daughter that I'm *never* going to know." He pointed at his cranium. "But I've still got this: my brain. I may never see my dad again, I may never stay up all night bullshitting with DK again, I may never hear Elvis again, but I'm *still* the guy who built *Farscape I*. Maybe it's not much compared to Moya or even your Prowler, but *I built it*. Even after all this time, I may not know a helluva lot about life in your end of the universe, but I *do* know how to fix Liantac's problem. The exhaust system in my module can be adjusted to repel the particles. This is *my* solution, Aeryn—nobody else could possibly come up with this because nobody around here has an Earth-style exhaust system in their ships. I am *not* gonna destroy one of the few things I can still claim as mine."

Aeryn's expression had changed from confusion to anger. "That's all well and good, Crichton, but what does it have to do with anything? Fine, you're separated from your home—is this supposed to elicit sympathy in me?"

"No, Aeryn, it—"

"We're *all* in the same situation, Crichton. Don't you dare sit there and tell me that your brand of suffering is somehow superior to mine or D'Argo's or Zhaan's!"

"D'Argo still sees the occasional Luxan or three, and at least he has a *chance* of seeing his kid again. Zhaan found a whole moon full of Delvians. Hell, Rygel still thinks he's got a shot at getting his throne back. And at least he can find out the lyrics to one of his Hynerian lullabies if he needs to!" Crichton was on his feet now, his voice rising. "And you still get to eat the same food, fly the same Prowler, see the same types of people you always have. Hell, you even get to bump into people you knew before! Best I can do is alien re-creations of home."

Aeryn stood up also. "So we're supposed to feel sorry for you, is that it? Poor, poor Crichton, he can't play with the same toys he used to play with, so let's indulge him. So what if the Peacekeepers spread their influence even further into the Uncharteds?"

"That's not what I meant!"

They were standing almost nose to nose now. "Look," Aeryn said, "maybe you have lost more than I have—but that's only because you had more in the first place!"

Crichton's retort caught in his throat, his anger quickly fading. He reached a hand towards Aeryn.

Aeryn turned away. "Don't," she said softly.

Crichton put his hand down.

She turned back to him. Her own expression had softened.

They stared at each other in silence. Crichton felt like a steamroller had suddenly gone into overdrive in his stomach.

"Lieutenant Asmat?"

Crichton did a double take at Aeryn's comm. *That's Sparky.*

Frowning, Aeryn tapped her comm. "This is Lieutenant Clow Asmat," she said slowly.

"This is Dominar Rygel XVI of the Hynerian Empire. We met at the Esher Hotel bar earlier."

"I remember. As I recall, I told you to frell off."

"Never mind that," Rygel said quickly. *"I understand that you're in negotiations with one of the Consortium members."*

"What makes you say that?"

Crichton shivered. Aeryn had put a frightening amount of menace into that simple question. He regarded her more closely. Her jaw was set differently, her eyes had narrowed, and her body had tensed. Aside from her still-unkempt hair, there was no sign of the drunken wreck he'd walked in on just a short time ago. *Right now, she's a one-hundred-percent USDA-approved Grade-A Peacekeeper commando*.

"*Information comes my way*," Rygel said smugly. "*In any case, I have a counteroffer for you from another member of the Consortium. A lady named Ornara wishes to speak—*"

"I'm not interested in anything you have to say, Dominar, nor in anything said by this Ornara person, nor any of the other decadent fahrbots in the Consortium. Do not ever contact me on this frequency again, or the Hynerians will be short one dominar."

She tapped her comm. As soon as she did, the mask fell. Her jaw lost its rigidity, her eyes softened, and her shoulders slumped a bit. Aeryn Sun—*my Aeryn Sun, that is*, Crichton thought, *as opposed to the Peacekeepers'*—was back. He couldn't help but grin. "Nice work. That ought to sour Ornara on the PKs."

"Let's hope so."

"Gotta give ol' King Buckwheat credit. He came through on that one."

"Perhaps. But we still—"

"*Crichton.*"

It was Rygel again, this time on Crichton's comm.

"What is it, Spanky?"

"*How dare you address me that way! Do that again, and I'll have you flogged.*" His voice became slightly more distant. "*I do apologize for my servant's manners, Ornara.*"

Grinning, Crichton said, "I'm dreadfully sorry, your worship. What can your humble servant do for your dominarness?"

"*That's better. I wanted to check on the status of that little project Netoros asked you to work on.*"

Not sure what answer Rygel was expecting, Crichton simply said, "It hasn't changed since the last time you checked in, your fluffiness."

"Have you shared your findings with Netoros yet?"

"Uh, not yet," Crichton said slowly.

"Excellent. Kindly don't. We have a better offer."

"Pardon my presumption, your officiousness, but isn't this part of fulfilling your debt to—"

"Don't question me, Crichton! Just meet me at the restaurant in Ornara's Emporium in an arn—and bring the specifics of the project with you. Is that understood?"

Trying not to laugh, Crichton said, "Perfectly, your royal heinie. See you in an arn." He tapped his comm and looked at Aeryn. "Methinks the Hynerian hath made a deal."

To Crichton's surprise, Aeryn actually returned the smile. "Looks like he hath, yes."

"Look, Aeryn, I'm sorry if I—"

"No, it's all right. I was, after all, rather drunk."

"Oh, *now* you admit it?"

Gesturing towards the bathroom, Aeryn said, "Well, after spending a quarter arn in there—what's that expression of yours?—puking my entrails out?"

"Close enough. Look, I'd better get going and see what Sparky's cooked up."

"Be careful, Crichton. Remember, this *is* Rygel. If he hasn't contrived to make matters worse, I will be stunned."

Shrugging, Crichton said, "Hey, what's the worst that can happen?"

"Do you really want me to answer that?"

"Not really, no," Crichton admitted. "I'll watch my back, don't worry. What's your plan?"

Again, Aeryn smiled, but this time it was a vicious smile. *Almost like her old self,* Crichton thought happily.

"I suspect Netoros is going to be very unhappy with the response she gets from me in the morning."

"Good," Crichton said, returning the smile. "Keep me posted."

"You too."

*   *   *

D'Argo had stood patiently while Zhaan recounted the
story of what happened to her at Garess's. None of it had
been much of a surprise—neither the attack, nor Zhaan's
way of handling it—but it still angered D'Argo that Zhaan
had had to be put through such trauma.

She had also given him the information Aeryn had provided via Rygel—that Netoros intended to sell them out to
the Peacekeepers.

When she finished, D'Argo said, "And of course that
Hynerian prabakto was nowhere to be found when you actually might have required his help."

"He would hardly have been of any assistance, D'Argo,"
Zhaan said in that maddeningly reasonable tone of voice
that she always used whenever she needed to defend Rygel
to D'Argo. *She uses that tone far too often*, he thought.

They stood backstage at the Harilear Club. Zhaan had
come to the door claiming to be a friend of Licit's bodyguard. The Sebacean bouncer had been skeptical—since
D'Argo's dramatic chase through the Casino, several people had claimed to be a friend of Licit's bodyguard—but
Zhaan had convinced him to check with D'Argo. Once he
vouched for her, everyone in the Harilear treated her like
family. She had been allowed backstage with D'Argo while
Licit performed his afternoon show.

"How long will Garess and his enforcer remain paralyzed?" D'Argo asked.

"I can't say for sure how a Lian's immune system will
respond to it. At a guess, at least fourteen arns. Thirteen
arns, now."

"Good. Plenty of time, then," D'Argo said with a smile.
"Come with me."

"Where are we going?" Zhaan asked.

"To contact someone who might be able to help us."

Zhaan's eyes narrowed. "Not Netoros?"

"No," D'Argo said. "Remember the sergeant who took
that Delvian into custody?"

"The one who tried to stop you after you had garbage thrown on you?" Zhaan said with a mischievous smile.

A look of disgust crossed D'Argo's face. "Do you know I *still* haven't gotten the smell out of my nostrils?"

Putting a comforting hand on D'Argo's shoulder, Zhaan said, "I have some herbs back on Moya that will clear your olfactory passages."

D'Argo nodded gratefully. "How is it that you always have a remedy for what ails us?"

"The same way you are always brave in the face of whatever adversity we face, sweet D'Argo. It is simply what I do."

Smiling once again, D'Argo nodded in acknowledgment as they left the backstage area. "In any case, this morning I went with Licit to the Security office to give the sergeant my statement on the chase from last night. The interesting thing was that Netoros had specifically requested that no criminal charges be filed against Holkom, but that he be remanded into her custody."

"But why—" Zhaan started, then she blinked. "Of course. Netoros is trying to curry favor with Garess. So she will provide him with a Delvian sample for his collection in this Holkom person."

"Exactly," D'Argo said. "You were provided solely to identify the last of his exotic plants—but she couldn't let him take you prisoner since she needs you available to be turned in to the Peacekeepers. So she had a substitute ready. It wouldn't surprise me if she engineered this entire charade with me and Licit just so that she'd have a Delvian to give Garess."

As they came out into the main tavern area, Zhaan asked, "How can this sergeant help us turn this to our advantage?"

"I don't think Netoros expected Garess to try to capture you so soon—if indeed she expected him to do so at all. And if she did expect it, I'm sure she thought Garess would succeed. After all, she does not know you as we do."

Zhaan smiled at that.

They approached the front desk of the Harilear. A short, fat, green-feathered Lian named Greeg was on duty. He wore a form-fitting one-piece suit that was ill-advised for someone of his girth.

"Hey there, D'Argo! What can I do for you and your lovely friend?"

Zhaan smiled at the compliment, but D'Argo didn't hide his annoyance. At first, Greeg had viewed D'Argo as little better than an insect. But since hearing about D'Argo's pursuit of Holkom, he now thought D'Argo was, as Crichton had said last night, "the coolest cat around."

"I need you to get in touch with Sergeant Oshay of Security."

"No problem, D'Argo."

The fat Lian pressed some buttons on his desk and spoke quietly into his headset. Then he removed the headset and handed it to D'Argo. "Sergeant Oshay is on the line."

D'Argo wiped off the headset and set it to privacy mode before putting it on. The privacy mode established a sound-impermeable forcefield around the wearer. As long as the connection was active, only the person on the other side would hear D'Argo's words. Greeg, meanwhile, rotated the screen on his desk so that D'Argo could see the face of the sergeant.

"You got something to add to your statement?" the sergeant asked angrily.

D'Argo had expected this reaction. Oshay was furious that charges had not been pressed against Holkom, as well as against D'Argo for firing on one of his officers.

"No," D'Argo replied, "but I do have some information about something else. A friend of mine has just come to me asking for help. She has also been working for Netoros—on her behalf, she went to the house of a man named Garess to identify some exotic plants for him."

"That's not surprising, is it? Those bloody plants are— well, never mind that. Why're you telling me this?"

"Because Garess assaulted my friend and tried to put her in his collection."

"I was right the first time I saw you. You are a loony. Why—"

"My friend is a Delvian."

Oshay straightened. *"A Delvian? What exactly happened?"*

"My friend—her name is Zhaan—can give you a full statement, which includes the involvement of Netoros in the whole plan."

The sergeant's eyes widened at that. *"Can she now?"*

"Yes."

There was another pause while, D'Argo presumed, Oshay weighed the relative merits of taking on two members of the Consortium.

"No harm in taking a statement is there? Bring her down."

"She will be there shortly. Thank you, Sergeant."

D'Argo turned the privacy mode off and handed the headset back to Greeg, then summoned the Sebacean bouncer. "I cannot leave Licit's side or Netoros will be alerted," he whispered to Zhaan. When the Sebacean arrived, he said, "My friend Zhaan needs to be escorted to the Security office. Can you take care of that for me?"

"Of course," he said with a quick nod. "Anything for you, D'Argo. I'll get Skot to cover for me."

Zhaan patted D'Argo's cheek and gave him a warm smile. "Thank you, sweet D'Argo."

"One way or another, Garess *will* pay for what he tried to do."

"Indeed."

She left with the bouncer. D'Argo returned backstage.

For once, this time Licit's songs didn't make him feel ill.

Greeg smiled as D'Argo walked off. He had listened in on D'Argo's entire conversation with that sergeant on his spare earpiece. Not the most legal thing to do, but he didn't think D'Argo was likely to take action against him.

Taking on the Consortium, huh? That takes some serious mivonks, he thought.

Telling Security about it was all well and good, but that wasn't where the money was. *Typical warrior type,* Greeg thought about D'Argo. *Only has a head for tactics, no brains at all for finance.*

Greeg, however, felt that he did have a head for finance. That was why he was going to go places. Sure, he'd had some setbacks, but they were minor—and once he paid off the last of that loan he'd had to take out after losing that Hranto tournament, he'd really be able to make a name for himself. *No more sitting at the front desk for me, no. I'm gonna be a* player.

He checked the directory for the hotline to the news service, then connected himself to it.

"Hotline," said a bored voice. It didn't even have a visual feed; the screen just showed the news service's logo.

"You guys still pay ten retri for hot tips?"

"If the tip is really hot, yeah."

"Well, how's a Delvian accusing two Consortium members of trying to imprison her qualify?"

The voice no longer sounded bored. *"You serious?"*

"Oh yeah. You know the Luxan who saved Licit's life? Well, he's got a friend . . ."

CHAPTER 12

With every new piece of information he got from Moya in the constant stream of mental communication that he received from the Leviathan, Pilot grew more concerned.

His four arms danced around the various controls that always sat in front of him—and always would, until he or Moya died. Some would question Pilot's sanity in choosing this lifestyle—to always remain in the same place, attached directly to the Leviathan through synaptic connections where his legs once were. At the very least, some might question his ability to remain sane in such a situation. After all, he could never leave his den, never even move from his place at the console. Some might see that as the worst kind of imprisonment.

But Pilot did not view himself as a prisoner. Quite the opposite, in fact—he was unfettered. He and Moya explored the infinite, and they had even been fortunate enough to do it in complete freedom rather than under the yoke of the Peacekeepers.

Freedom, of course, came at a price. Right now, that price was getting more expensive. Slowly but surely, each of Moya's systems was slowing down. Pilot had calculated that within another twelve arns, all of her functions would be at half speed or worse. As long as they remained in a standard orbit, there was less cause for panic, but if the ship was forced to make any sudden maneuvers . . .

Of course, there was a limit to the amount of maneuvering they could do, since the ship could not increase its altitude relative to Liantac by more than a hundred metras without flying full into the Clorium field. In which case, Moya would be completely crippled.

Pilot could feel Moya's growing concern. If he tried to put the feeling into words to the others, he could not. He had attempted to explain it to D'Argo, during the trying time when Pilot's mind somehow wound up in Chiana's body and D'Argo was in Pilot's. He had managed to talk the Luxan through it, but the words he used were nowhere near adequate to describe the depth of his connection to Moya.

He opened a signal to Chiana. The Nebari was presently in the Command, muttering to herself. "*—don't see why I have to be stuck up here with Pilot and the frelling DRDs when I could be down there having fun. I'll bet Rygel's having a wonderful time.*"

"Chiana."

"*Yes, Pilot?*"

"Moya wishes to give the techno-organic ferry that we took on board a proper funeral."

"*What?*"

Pilot struggled with the words to express Moya's desires. It was sometimes difficult. "Moya feels a—kinship with the ferry and mourns its loss. She'd like to release it and allow its orbit to decay. It is of sufficiently small mass that it will burn up as it does so."

"*Fine by me,*" Chiana said. "*That thing is just stinking up the hangar anyhow.*"

"Moya would also like you to say a few words in memoriam." The Leviathan, too, had heard Chiana's words, and Pilot had to admit to a certain amusement at Moya's request.

"Me?"

"Yes, Chiana, you."

Chiana stammered. *"This is the sort of thing Zhaan does. I mean, you know—she's a priest. She probably gives these kinds of speeches all the time. But not me. I mean—"*

"Moya has thought very highly of you ever since you helped her through Talyn's birth. She can think of no better person to speak for the deceased vessel." He hesitated. "Besides—there is no one else available."

There was silence on the other end, though Pilot could hear Chiana breathing.

"We realize that this may not be an improvement over being stuck on the ship with myself and the DRDs," Pilot added.

"What? Oh! Uh, look, Pilot, I didn't mean—"

"I understand, Chiana," Pilot said, in a soothing tone. "Liantac is, I'm sure, a very exciting place for someone of your—temperament. We appreciate that you have stayed behind to be with Moya and me during this crisis. She is very scared. Perhaps this funeral will take her mind off the increasing danger from the Clorium field and the larik particles."

Pilot was pleased to hear the contrite tone in Chiana's voice as she said, *"Pilot, tell Moya I'm sorry. Truly. I'd—."* A long hesitation. *"I'd be honored to give a eulogy for the ferry."*

"Thank you, Chiana."

Accompanied by several of the DRDs, Chiana hurried to the hangar. Pilot set his visual feed to watch them. The look on Chiana's face showed all too clearly how she felt about the awful smell of the rotted ferry.

Idly, Pilot wondered what the smell was like. His den generally had the same look and smell, except when something went horribly wrong. Still, given the look of disgust on Chiana's face right now, it was probably for the best that odors did not transmit over the intercom.

"Uh, well, I guess this is where I say something, huh?" Chiana finally said. *"Well, this ship was, uh—a very good ship. It had a very important purpose in life—to bring people to and from this planet when there was—well, there was no other way to do it, really. It, ah, it ended its life— okay, it died—trying to fulfill its function one last time. And, uh, it almost made it. Kind of. I mean, it tried its best, you know? It lived a full life, and it, uh . . ."* Chiana paused and looked directly at the ferry. *"Yeah, it lived a full life and it ended its life helping people to—y'know, to go someplace for fun, to get to a place where they would enjoy themselves. After all, that's what Liantac is all about, right?"* She smiled nervously. *"I mean, that's why people come here—to have fun. And this ship was just trying to bring people pleasure. What better calling could you have than that, right?"*

Chiana hesitated, looked up at the ceiling for a moment, then went on. *"It's hard to find someone like you and then lose them. Especially when you know there aren't a lot of others like you. It's rough, y'know? But at least—at least we're able to give this ship a proper goodbye."*

After pausing to wipe a tear from her eye, Chiana said, *"If Zhaan were here, she'd say something really profound."* She laughed quickly. *"I've never been much for that, so I'll just say—well, if living ships have an afterlife, I hope that this ship is happy there. Safe journey.*

"Okay, Pilot, go ahead."

Pilot nodded. He closed the door with his outer right arm, then decompressed the hangar with his inner right arm, all the while using his inner left arm to set the docking web to expel the ferry as soon as the decompression sequence was complete.

Soon, the rotted ferry had cleared the hangar and was orbiting around Liantac. "According to the readings," Pilot told Chiana, "the ferry will complete its decay in a little over one solar day and then burn up in the atmosphere. Moya and I both feel that it is a fitting way for it to go.

Moya enjoyed your eulogy, Chiana," he added, sharing that thought of the Leviathan's.

"You don't have to lie to me, Pilot. That has to have been the worst eulogy on record."

"Not at all," Pilot said sincerely. "It was truly heartfelt. Even Zhaan could not have done better."

Chiana broke into a grin. *"You mean that?"*

"Of course."

"Huh. Well, thank you, Pilot, and thank you, Moya."

"You're welcome, Chiana. And—" He hesitated. While neither he nor Moya wanted to be left alone, they both knew how much Chiana wanted to be on Liantac with the rest of the crew. "If you wish to take another transport pod to the planet, we would not object."

"Really?" Chiana said, her eyes widening. Then her face relaxed again, and she smiled. *"Thanks, but—I think I'll stay up here and keep you company. I know Moya's worried about the Clorium field, and I wouldn't want to leave her now."*

"We are both grateful to you, Chiana."

"Don't mention it. How is Moya holding up, anyhow?"

"Her systems are growing more unresponsive," Pilot said. He ran several scans, and they all told him the same thing: the ship needed to get away from this Clorium field soon.

"Well, I hope the gang can pull off whatever they're going to pull off soon."

"So do I," Pilot said. "I don't know how much longer I can compensate for the Clorium field before the larik particles become a serious problem."

"Keep me posted, okay, Pilot?"

"Of course."

"And let the others know, too." She smiled a lopsided smile. *"No sense in you and me being the only ones worrying."*

Pilot returned the smile. "No indeed."

*   *   *

"It's about time you arrived, Crichton."

Crichton, led into the restaurant by a tall, blue-feathered Lian, resisted the urge to smack Rygel on the head. After all, he was, he reminded himself, supposed to be Rygel's humble servant. *Maybe I'll give him the whuppin' he deserves when this is all over and he least expects it,* he thought, with some satisfaction.

Rygel was stuffing his face, as usual. Opposite him sat a Lian female whom Crichton swore was the spitting image of Roseanne, if the heavy-set actress had had short white feathers and a beak. She was pecking away at some kind of fruit cocktail—at least Crichton assumed it was fruit, though fruit didn't come in turquoise back home.

"I got here as fast as I could, your royal studliness. And before you ask," he held up the chip that contained all the data on his larik particle research, "here's most of the information you'll need."

Indignantly, Rygel said, "Most? Where's the rest?"

"On Moya right now. It's in my module."

"What, *that* useless piece of dren?"

"That useless piece of dren is the key to solving all of Liantac's problems."

The Lian chimed in. "Is it, now?"

Damn, Crichton thought, *she's as loud as Roseanne, too.*

"Crichton, this is Ornara. Like Netoros, she's a member of the Consortium. Unlike Netoros, she understands how to do business in a civilized manner."

"Well, more civilized, anyhow," she said with a booming laugh. "Please have a seat, Crichton."

Reluctantly, Crichton took the seat between Rygel and Ornara, wondering if it was really safe to be flanked by these two.

"So, Rygel tells me that Netoros wanted you to come up with a solution to the larik problem—and you have!"

Inching his chair a bit closer to Rygel, Crichton thought, *It's definitely not safe for my eardrums. This woman's got herself a strong set of pipes.* Aloud, he said, "That's right.

And it's not a solution you're likely to find from anyone else."

Blue Feathers came back. "Excuse me for interrupting, ma'am, but something has just been broadcast on the news service that I think you need to see right away. I took the liberty of bringing a recording of it."

"I'm in the midst of a meeting, Rolin! Can't this wait?"

"No, ma'am, it cannot."

Ornara seemed taken aback by that response. "All right, then, let's see it."

Rolin placed an oblong block on the table, then pressed a button. A tiny hologram of a Lian with remarkably well-groomed teal feathers appeared.

If she says, "Help me, Obi-Wan," I'm so outta here, Crichton thought with a smile.

In a soothing voice, the hologram said, *"We have learned that Security has arrested Consortium member Garess as well as an unnamed associate."*

As she spoke, the head of a male Lian appeared over her head and rotated so that the face could be seen from all sides. Crichton assumed that it was Garess.

"Allegedly, a complaint was made to Security by an as-yet-unidentified Delvian, who claimed that Garess—a known collector of exotic flora—wished to add the Delvian to his collection. The Delvian also claims to have been sent to Garess by another Consortium member, Netoros."

At that, the image over the newscaster's head changed to that of Netoros.

"As yet, there is no comment from either Netoros or Garess. Sources indicate that the unnamed Delvian is associated in some way with Ka D'Argo, the Luxan who saved famed singer Licit from a Delvian attacker yesterday."

At the mention of D'Argo's name, the image changed to that of another Lian. Crichton recognized him as Licit from the various advertisements he'd seen for the Harilear Club around the Casino. *Guess they didn't have any pics of D'Argo. Pity—his scowl would make for good TV.*

The newscaster continued. *"It is also possible that the*

Delvian who made the complaint is the same one who attacked Licit, as sources within Security have confirmed that that Delvian, a man named Holkom, was not charged, but remanded to Netoros's custody this morning. More on this story as it develops."

Rolin shut the viewer off.

Ornara's tiny eyes narrowed even further as she looked at Rygel. "Interesting. Netoros makes deals with Peacekeepers and sends Delvians to be captured. This is *not* good for business." She picked up her napkin, dabbed her beak, then threw it down in disgust. "We cannot afford this kind of scandal now!" she bellowed. Crichton was sure he had heard glass rattle.

Rygel, who had spent the time since Rolin showed up with the newscast wolfing down one of the many delicacies he had ordered, finally spoke up. "Perhaps not, but the best way to bury a scandal is to publicize some good news— say, the announcement of a new procedure to allow *all* ships to come to Liantac once again?"

"It, uh, isn't a universal solution," Crichton said quickly, not wanting Ornara to get her hopes up *too* high. "It'll require replacing the entire exhaust system in a ship. But at the very least, you can run a ferry service that isn't in danger of rotting out from under you."

"And this process works?"

Crichton tipped his head to the side. "Well, in theory. I haven't had the chance to test it yet, although that won't take too long. But all the sims say it'll work."

Ornara let loose with another belly-shaking laugh and said, "Simulations of Hranto games show that every player has an equal chance of winning, but the winnings aren't usually divided evenly."

"Maybe not," said Crichton, "but I have faith in my ship."

"And we are willing to sell you the exclusive rights to this new exhaust system," added Rygel.

"I'm sure you are," Ornara said, leaning back in her chair

and resting her long arms on her ample belly. "The question is: am I willing to pay the price you name?"

Rygel pushed his plate aside and moved a bowl of purple fruit drenched in blue cream in front of him. "Then let us discuss terms, shall we? First of all, I want this collar off. You will either pay off my debt directly to Netoros or give me enough to pay her. The amount in the pot was eight thousand nine hundred and forty-five retri; Netoros valued Moya at an additional four thousand."

Another teeth-jangling laugh. "You truly think this Sebacean's breakthrough is worth almost thirteen thousand retri?"

Crichton sighed. *No point in telling her I'm not Sebacean. It'd take way too long to explain that one.*

"No, as it happens, I don't." Rygel consumed some fruit, wiped his mouth with his sleeve, and then continued: "It's worth considerably more than that—and you know it."

"Perhaps." Ornara leaned forward and lapped up some steaming red liquid in a bowl. "I'm not inclined to give Netoros any cash given her behavior—on the other hand, she'll probably need it for her legal fees. What more do you require?"

"Your promise, in writing, that Liantac will always be a safe haven for me, my ship, and my servants—and special service at all of the casinos."

Crichton rolled his eyes. He was now getting hungry watching these two and looked around for a waiter.

Chuckling, Ornara said, "I can only make that guarantee for myself and the properties that I own—and that will only hold true for as long as I am a member of the Consortium."

"Fair enough."

"One more thing," Crichton said, remembering Netoros's rather impressive intelligence-gathering efforts.

"The servant speaks?" Ornara said with amusement.

Ignoring the comment, Crichton quoted Netoros's line at Ornara: "The only people who talk more than gamblers are drunks, and you get plenty of those in here. We want you to keep your ears open for any information about the movements of a Peacekeeper named Scorpius or of the where-abouts of a half-Luxan half-Sebacean boy named Jothee. We'll leave you one of our comm units—you can contact us on one of them. It may take a while to reach us, but we'll hear it eventually."

"I can understand about the Peacekeeper, but why the interest in a half-breed boy?"

"That is none of your business," Crichton said. "One more thing."

"Another?" Ornara's tiny eyes opened as wide as they could go. "You are starting to overvalue your work, Crichton."

"This is small—can you get a waiter over here? I'm *starving*."

Ornara laughed loudly enough to make her past guffaws seem like tiny chuckles. This time the nearby glassware definitely rattled.

She summoned a waiter, then turned to Rygel. "Dominar, assuming your servant's test is successful, you have yourself a deal."

In something like a state of shock, Netoros stared at the image of the newscaster on the holographic projector in her office.

She then pushed a button and backtracked the recording to the beginning of the news story.

Once again, the newscaster described the arrest of Garess.

"This is a frelling nightmare," she muttered, then pushed the intercom button. "Celong, get in here."

When Celong entered, Netoros indicated the image of the newscaster. "Did you know that Garess's little disaster has made the news?"

"Yes. In fact, several representatives of the news service have been calling. I have told them that you're unavailable and will call back as soon as you can."

Not for the first time, Netoros thanked Thori for the efficiency and perspicacity of her assistant. "Good work."

The newscaster got to the part where D'Argo was mentioned. "And that damned Luxan—I go and make him a celebrity, and this is the thanks I get. How is Holkom, by the way?"

"Still under heavy sedation. By the way, Sergeant Oshay has continued to call. I've been putting him off, but he's getting insistent. With this news report, I'm not sure your influence will be as—ah—meaningful."

"Probably not," Netoros said with a sigh. "That Garess is a fool."

Celong's eyes narrowed. "We did anticipate that Garess might try to stick Zhaan in one of his cages before we had a chance to deliver Holkom to him."

"Yes, but I didn't expect Zhaan to escape. From what I've heard, she overpowered them in an instant. She's a *priest*, for Thori's sake." Again, Netoros sighed. "I should have listened to my own advice. These people have evaded the Peacekeepers for two cycles. They're much more resourceful than even I gave them credit for."

"They all are. Dominar Rygel was sighted going into Ornara's Emporium and playing at her Haunan table. Oh, and Commander Crichton has disappeared."

"What?" Netoros did not need this on top of everything else.

"He took a break over two arns ago, and he hasn't come back. He also wiped all his work from the computer."

Pounding her desk, Netoros said, "Damn him!" Crichton was, in many ways, the most valuable member of Moya's crew. True, the Peacekeepers would still want their three prisoners back, but they were a much lower priority. Crichton, on the other hand, was wanted by a high-ranking member of the scientific division. She needed him more than the others.

Netoros closed her eyes, took a deep breath, and looked up at Celong. "Find Crichton. I don't care what it takes, but get him back here."

Celong nodded. "Right away."

About fifteen microts after she left the office, Celong

contacted her on the intercom. *"You have a call from Ornara."*

"I can't talk to her right now. Tell her people that—"

"Netoros, this isn't from one of her people, it's directly from Ornara."

"Oh, Thori's beak." Netoros toyed with the idea of refusing the call. *But no, that would be suicidal right now.* "Put her through, Celong."

A hologram of Ornara's face appeared over Netoros's desk. *"Greetings, Netoros!"* she said in her sonic boom of a voice. *"How are you this fine day?"*

Discreetly turning down the volume on the receiver, Netoros replied, "A bit busy. I'm sorry about rescheduling tomorrow's meeting, but—"

"Oh, don't worry about that, my dear, don't worry at all! I'm sure you'll be far too busy. I just wanted to let you know that I just transferred thirteen thousand retri to your account on behalf of Dominar Rygel XVI."

Netoros felt the blood drain from her face. "I beg your pardon?"

"The dominar owed you twelve thousand nine hundred and forty-five retri. Consider the additional fifty-five retri a gift—or a contribution to your legal defense fund," Ornara added with more than a little smugness.

"I'm—stunned by your generosity."

Ornara tipped her head to the side. *"It's just business, Netoros. I should think you'd be more stunned by the behavior of your good friend Garess."*

"That too was just business, Ornara," Netoros said tightly. "If there's nothing else, I have a great deal of work to do."

"Of course. Oh, and I've registered this transaction with the central computer, so the dominar's collar has been deactivated. I assume he'll come by to have it removed by one of your people at some point."

"He's welcome to come by here at any time." *If he does, I'll lock him in a frelling closet,* Netoros thought angrily.

"Excellent. Oh, and I assume you'll be taking that annoying Clorium field down. I know that it's harmless except to Leviathans but—well, it's off-putting. Makes people nervous, you understand."

"I'll have it taken care of right away."

"See that you do. Well, much as I would love to continue chatting, I too have business to attend to, my dear. Goodbye!"

As soon as Ornara's face disappeared, Netoros walked over to the shelf containing an impressive array of alcoholic beverages. She poured herself a raslak and lapped it all up. Then she poured another. And another.

Finally, she touched the intercom. "Celong, contact Lieutenant Asmat and get her over here. I can't wait until tomorrow to get her answer."

"Right away."

Netoros stared through her window at the bright lights of the Casino, including dozens of advertisements for establishments she owned. All her life, she'd wanted this. To be in power. Her present plan was one that would make her the *only* one in power. It had been expensive and risky—there had been no guarantee that Rari would find the Leviathan, there was the chance that the information she had on its occupants was either inaccurate or out of date, and there was the possibility that the Hynerian would not take the numerous enticements she'd set in his path to come to the House of Games. It had been a gamble, true, but Netoros had always been a skilled gambler—that was how she had gained the power she had already.

And it did work. Every single frelling bit of it. So how has everything now gone so horrendously wrong?

Celong's voice sounded over the intercom. *"Lieutenant Asmat is here."*

"Good. Send her in."

Asmat entered, looking as unpleasant as ever. "What do you want?" she asked rudely.

"I'm afraid the situation has changed somewhat. I need your down payment right away so I can start buying out—"

"Yes, the situation has changed rather dramatically," Asmat interrupted. "I was under the impression that you had control over the crew of the Leviathan."

"I—"

"According to the news report I just saw, Zotoh Zhaan is no longer with Garess—indeed, Garess himself is under arrest. Tell me, where is she now?"

Netoros started to answer, but realized that there was nothing she could say that would make the situation any better. She had no idea where Zhaan was, and to lie would be a critical error. So she stayed silent.

Asmat continued. "According to the public records on your central computer, which I was perusing when your assistant called me here, Dominar Rygel's debt has been paid—which, I assume, means he is no longer wearing the debtor's collar?"

"Well, actually, he is still wearing it," Netoros said. *Damn her for checking the records!* They were available for the general public to view, of course, but who would have ever thought that Asmat would know such a thing?

"But it's been deactivated, has it not?"

"Yes," Netoros was forced to admit.

"So that leaves Commander Crichton and Ka D'Argo. You said Crichton was in one of your offices here. Take me to him."

"Commander Crichton has taken a break. He'll be back shortly."

"Of course he will." Asmat picked up the bottle of raslak that Netoros had almost drained. "The fact is, Netoros, you don't have three of the four prisoners you promised me— just the Luxan. I don't like Luxans, Netoros. They're loud and obnoxious and hard to handle." She took a gulp from the bottle. "As for the Leviathan—*I* have one of its transport pods. Therefore I can take it whenever I please."

Netoros seethed, but said nothing.

"You don't have control of the prisoners, you don't have control of the Leviathan, and without my down payment, you don't have control of Liantac. You, in fact, have nothing."

The lieutenant set the bottle down, and moved close to Netoros. "As far as the Peacekeepers are concerned, Netoros, this negotiation is over. Don't ever contact us again, or you'll live to regret it."

With that, Asmat stalked out of the office.

Netoros finished the bottle of raslak, then hurled it across the room.

Celong's voice sounded once again on the intercom. *"Sergeant Oshay is here to see you, Netoros. He insists that he be allowed to see you now."*

Yet again, Netoros sighed. "Send him in."

CHAPTER 13

"Yeeeeeeeeeeeeeeeeeee-haw!"

"I assume that means that the test was a success?" said D'Argo.

"You bet your bippy, D'Argo. Farscape I is on course and steady with nary a trace of larik particle contamination in the engine."

Aeryn shook her head. She stood in the Command on Moya with D'Argo and Chiana, Pilot's holographic image visible on its usual screen. Zhaan was putting away the herbs Chiana had purchased for her on Liantac. Rygel had remained on the surface until after Crichton performed his test as a goodwill gesture. (A gesture that Ornara had insisted on, and to which Rygel had only agreed under loud protest.) Crichton had spent several arns adjusting the exhaust system of his module, then had taken it out. Now it seemed that his theory was indeed correct.

Aeryn understood how much it meant to Crichton to prove that his solution worked, and she was truly happy for him that it did. *But I can't help feeling that this is a mistake, and that Liantac's recovery will just bring the Peacekeepers back that much sooner.*

However, none of the others felt the same way, and besides, it did provide an immediate solution to getting off this frelling planet.

Crichton continued, *"Pilot, I'm gonna do a full orbit, then head on back, all right?"*

"Of course, Commander," Pilot said. *"The docking web is standing by."*

"Great. Headin' around to the other side of the planet. I'll talk to you guys when I come back around agai—" Crichton's signal deteriorated as he circled around the far side of the planet, then gave out altogether. The Leviathan was in a slow parking orbit as opposed to the high-speed orbital posture Crichton had taken.

"Pilot," D'Argo said, "has the Clorium field dissipated yet?"

"No. Based on current scans, I'd say that it will take at least sixteen arns for it to have dissipated enough for it to be safe for Moya to traverse it. And it isn't happening a moment too soon. I fear for what might have occurred if we had remained proximate to the Clorium field at full strength for any longer."

"The microt that Moya feels safe, leave orbit," D'Argo said. "I want to be away from this frelling planet as soon as possible."

"I agree," Aeryn said. "We never should have come here in the first place."

"Why do you say that?" Chiana said. "We got supplies we wouldn't have gotten otherwise, we got a good pile of cash, and we stopped the Peacekeepers from taking over. I'd say that's a pretty good day's work, wouldn't you?"

"I don't believe it was worth putting Moya, Zhaan, and D'Argo in harm's way."

D'Argo snorted. "I was never in any serious danger, Aeryn. Holkom was hardly a worthy foe and—"

"I'm sorry to interrupt," Pilot said, *"but I'm getting some strange readings from the techno-organic ferry."*

Aeryn frowned. "Isn't it still in the hold?"

"No," Chiana said. "Moya wanted to give it a proper funeral, so Pilot and I sent it out to burn up in a decaying orbit."

"All right," Aeryn said, confused. She didn't see the point, but she supposed that Moya had her reasons—*probably the same reason that she insisted on rescuing the ship in the first place.* "What kind of readings, Pilot?"

"I'm not sure. When the ferry entered the upper atmosphere, it started to emit a signal. I don't recognize the type, but it appears to be broadcasting on a Peacekeeper frequency."

Aeryn had an idea about what that signal might portend. As she walked over to one of the consoles, a cold feeling spread through her stomach. "Pipe the signal to this station, Pilot."

As soon as she saw the pulse of the signal on the screen in front of her and heard it on the speakers, Aeryn knew that her guess was correct. "It's a Peacekeeper Cleanser Bomb."

"What's that?" Chiana asked.

"We must leave orbit immediately," D'Argo said.

"We cannot," Pilot said. *"The Clorium field is not sufficiently dissipated."*

"Can't you compensate?" Aeryn asked.

"No. If Moya passes through the field now, she will be too numbed to function properly."

"What's a Peacekeeper Cleanser Bomb?" Chiana asked again, more insistently.

"A bomb that releases a biological agent that consumes any life-sustaining atmosphere," answered Aeryn. "Asmat must have brought it with her."

"Why would she do that?" Chiana asked.

D'Argo snarled. "The Peacekeepers have probably deemed this world worthy of being destroyed."

Aeryn shook her head. "No, the Cleansers are only used as a last resort. She must have been given instructions to use it if the negotiations failed. Pilot, you said the signal went active when it entered the upper atmosphere?"

"Yes."

"That fits. Extreme heat activates them. If I'm reading this signal correctly, we have less than two arns before this planet is stripped of its biosphere."

"Will it affect us?" Chiana asked, now sounding panicky.

Aeryn shrugged. "I don't know. I've only seen a Cleanser in action once, and there weren't any ships in orbit when it was activated. I wouldn't want to risk it, though."

"You have to disarm it," D'Argo said to Aeryn.

"Me? D'Argo, that's tech work. I was a commando, remember? I don't have the first clue how to disarm one of those things."

"Then we're dead."

"Honey, I'm hooooooome," Crichton said. Aeryn looked up at the screen to see his module crossing the terminator and coming into sight.

"Crichton," she said, "we have a new problem." She quickly filled him in.

"All right, then we need a tech to fix it. Luckily, we got one."

Frowning, Aeryn said, "What're you talking about?"

"How soon you forget. Stran, the PK tech. Remember? He ought to be able to disarm that thing."

Aeryn closed her eyes. *I should have remembered that. But how do we ask a man I disgraced for help? I knew we shouldn't have come to this planet.*

"You'll have to go down and talk to him, Crichton," she said.

"Me? Aeryn, he doesn't know me from Adam. It needs to be you or Pip."

"I'll go," Chiana quickly agreed. "Stran actually *likes* me."

"Of course, he does. He doesn't know you," Aeryn muttered.

Crichton said, *"Can we please save the catfight for later when I can enjoy it? Pilot, put out the docking web, I'm coming in."*

"Of course, Commander," Pilot said. *"But may I say that it should be Officer Sun who fetches Technician Stran."*

This took Aeryn aback. "Why?"

"Because you will need to go straight from Liantac's surface to the ferry's position in order to arrive in enough time to disarm the bomb. Matching course with the ferry in the upper atmosphere will require a pilot of great skill. The wind shear at that altitude will test the skills of even the finest pilot. So you can see, Officer Sun, you would be the most appropriate crew member to go."

Aeryn wanted to protest. She did not want to face Stran again. *Must I constantly be reminded of my past?*

But she knew Pilot was right. She was the only person on Moya with sufficient piloting skills to handle the task. No matter to whom she gave her allegiance, Aeryn Sun had always been a creature of duty, and right now, her duty was to save Liantac—and Moya—from the Cleanser.

"I'll take the transport pod," she said, quickly exiting the Command.

Eff Stran leaned back and stretched after the Sheyang customer left. *Finally, I've unloaded that frelling box of stembolts.* He'd been trying to get rid of those things for a cycle. Now, however, it was all arranged for delivery to that Sheyang's hotel room in the morning.

He looked around his store. The number of items strewn about the floor had actually been fairly well depleted over the last couple of days—he could almost clear a *second* path to the door, which he hadn't been able to do in quite some time. And it was mostly thanks to Chiana and ex-Officer Aeryn Sun.

"Oh how I like the sound of that," he said aloud to his empty store. "Ex-Officer Aeryn Sun. Just rolls off the tongue: ex-Officer Aeryn Sun."

With a rattle of beads, the voice of the female Stran hated most in the universe said, "I'm glad my status gives you such pleasure."

"Well, well, well, if it isn't *ex*-Officer Aeryn Sun." To

Stran's surprise, she was now wearing the uniform of a Peacekeeper lieutenant rather than the clothes she'd had on before. "Or is it still ex? Looks like you're not only back in, you've been promoted!"

"These clothes aren't mine," Aeryn said quickly. "I've been posing as a lieutenant, but that's not important right now."

"Oh, I'm sure it isn't. So, what brings you to my used parts emporium? Come to gloat over your handiwork? Or perhaps you want to swap stories about how we each got kicked out of the Peacekeepers?"

"Look, Stran, I know you hate me and if you still want to kill me, do it later, all right? Right now, I need your help. And so does the rest of this planet."

"What're you talking about?"

"You know that Peacekeeper presence you warned Chiana about?"

"Yeah?"

"Well, it showed up in the form of a lieutenant named Clow Asmat. She's dead now—she's the one I've been impersonating. Unfortunately, she brought a Cleanser Bomb with her."

The stew he'd had for lunch started to rumble towards Stran's throat. "You're joking."

"I wouldn't joke about that, believe me. Right now, it's in a decaying orbit aboard the techno-organic ferry that brought Asmat here, and it'll go off in a little over an arn."

Stran remembered the first time he'd studied the specs on a Cleanser. He hadn't been able to hold down food for two solar days afterward. "How the satra did it go active?"

"Friction from the atmospheric entry, most likely. Can you disarm it?"

"I can't believe it," Stran said, staring down at the floor in disbelief. "They'd actually wipe out—"

"Stran! Can you disarm it?"

He looked up at her. "Once a commando, always a commando, eh, Officer Sun?" He took a breath. "I think I can disarm it, yeah."

"Good. Let's go."

"Where?"

"My transport pod. It's from Moya, so it won't be affected by the larik particles."

He nodded. "Good. I was worried we'd be going up in one of those frelling ferries. I hate those things. Hang on, I need to get my tools."

As Stran assembled his tools, he tried to keep his hands from shaking. *A Cleanser Bomb. Who would do something like that?* Shaking his head and chuckling a most bitter chuckle, he answered himself, *The Peacekeepers, that's who, you welnitz. As if you needed any more proof that they're insane.*

Closing the lid on his toolkit, he hurried outside where Aeryn was waiting.

To Stran's shock, the transport pod was parked in the middle of the concourse. "How the frell did you get permission to land that thing *here*?" Then he noticed the small badge on the pod's hatchway entrance, which was adorned with the logo of Ornara. "You got permission from the Consortium?"

"What can I tell you, Stran," Aeryn said with a wry smile, "we have friends in high places. Let's go."

In microts they were heading up through the atmosphere. "There's a spacesuit in the back," said Aeryn. "You'll need that—the ferry's been completely exposed, so it won't be easy to breathe. Plus, it'll regulate your body temperature against the heat of atmospheric entry, and you'll need the magnetized boots to maintain your footing in that wind shear."

"Great. Delicate work in heavy winds and high heat while wearing bulky gloves. Anything else you want to do to complicate this?"

"I think that'll do for now," Aeryn replied.

As he climbed into the spacesuit, Stran said, "You know, it's ironic. I always loved the Peacekeepers. I believed in what we were doing, had no problem with doing my duty. I mean, yeah, there were problems—we were understaffed, overworked, underpaid. But that's normal." After fastening the main part of the suit, he looked around. "Where are the boots for this thing?"

"They should be in the locker."

"Well, they're not," Stran said, examining the locker more closely. He picked up the helmet, which revealed the boots. "No, wait, here they are. So, anyhow, I loved it. We did some good work. Then you came along and told me that the Fantir Regiment were traitors—as if I was supposed to know that." He pulled the boots on. "Once they kicked me out, though, that's when I finally stopped believing in it. How could I? I wasn't worth dren to them. Fantir probably realized that when they went rogue."

He grabbed an analyzer, set it to scan for a Cleanser's signal, then attached it to his belt. After that, he pulled on the gloves, and settled in the copilot's seat next to Aeryn. "I was exiled from Peacekeeper space for an act I didn't commit, but would gladly do now. Ironic, isn't it?"

Aeryn looked at him—and for the first time, Stran could see the pain in her eyes.

"I know how you feel," she said quietly.

She turned back to the controls.

"Yes," he said quietly, "I suppose you do."

"All right, we're pulling alongside the ferry now. Get ready."

"Right." Stran moved to the airlock. Waving his gloved hand over the sensor, it opened. He stepped inside and attached the tether to his belt. This would keep him attached to the transport pod no matter what happened. Then he walked over to the control panel and started the decompression procedure.

Haven't done this in cycles, but it's all coming back to me. I guess once a tech, always a tech, too.

Aeryn had lined the two ships up perfectly. Stran was impressed with her skill. He could feel the wind pounding against his spacesuit, and he hadn't even stepped out of the airlock yet.

Only about two metras separated the airlock from a very

large hole in the hull of the ferry. He activated the minijets in the boots that would propel him toward the hole.

The wind battered him almost senseless. It only took about three microts for him to bridge the distance, but he felt like he'd done a two-hundred-zacron run while getting beaten up by a Luxan. He stood in the remains of the ferry for a moment to catch his breath, and also to activate the magnetizers in the boots to keep himself rooted. Then he removed the analyzer from his belt and turned it on.

Suddenly, he was yanked upward, then back down again. As he collided with the fleshy bulkhead, he somehow managed to keep his grip on the analyzer.

"Careful, will you?" he said to Aeryn over the comm. "Almost yanked me out of the frelling ship, there."

"Sorry. Hit an updraft. Turn on the magnetizers on the boots."

"I did," he said angrily. "Either your updraft was too strong or your magnetizers aren't up to standard."

"Have you found the bomb?"

He looked at the readout. It was giving a signal, so it was definitely nearby. "Not yet. The analyzer says it's here, though. Hang on."

"We're between two windstreams now, so things will be calm for a bit."

"See if you can keep us here," Stran said as he moved aside what appeared to be the passenger seat. Under it sat a small bag. "Ah, here we go."

He opened the bag, and saw something both familiar—and unfamiliar.

"Oh, frell."

"What?"

"They changed the design. The good news is that I think I can still disarm it. The bad news is that I'm not sure I can do it in a hundred microts—which is all that's left on the timer."

"What? We should have at least a quarter of an arn left!"

"I told you," Stran said as he looked for the latch to open

the casing, "they redesigned it. If I don't figure out how to disarm this thing, we're all dead."

As he struggled with the casing, Aeryn said, *"Maybe not all. Moya might at least be able to escape."*

"With a Clorium field in place? Not bloody likely."

"I have to warn them at least," Aeryn said with a passion that surprised Stran. Then he heard a beeping sound. *"Pilot, is there any way Moya can get through the Clorium field?"*

A gentle voice said, *"It would not be advisable."*

"This bomb is going to go off in less than a hundred microts. You've got to get out of orbit now."

A deep voice then came on. *"Can't your tech friend disarm it?"*

Stran recognized it as the Luxan he had met briefly. *Come and disarm it yourself, you bartantic,* he thought angrily as he finally pried the casing off.

Eighty microts.

"He's trying," Aeryn said, *"but they've redesigned the Cleanser. He might not be able to. You've got to save yourselves."*

Yet another voice came on—this one with a peculiar accent. *"We're not leaving without you, Aeryn."*

"There isn't time, Crichton. I can't get back to Moya that fast. Get out of here while you still can. Pilot, can you StarBurst while you're still under the Clorium field?"

"In order to properly StarBurst, Moya needs to attain at least some forward velocity. It would mean initiating the StarBurst from the middle of the Clorium field. It could kill her."

"So could this bomb."

Stran didn't get it. Officer Aeryn Sun didn't give a krag's ass about anyone. Stran's own pleas cycles ago that he was only following orders had fallen on deaf ears.

Now, though, she was practically pleading with these people to save themselves and let her and Stran die. More peculiarly, the crew on that Leviathan seemed to care

enough about her not to want to abandon the two of them
to their death.

Death. Sobering thought, that. Still, it wasn't as if Stran
had a choice. There was indeed insufficient time to reach
the Leviathan—or any place else—before the bomb went
off. *If I don't disarm this thing, we're all for it—me, ex-
Officer Sun, and everyone on Liantac,* he thought.

Sixty-five microts.

The controls on the Cleanser were too small to operate
with gloved hands, so Stran took them off.

"Aaaaaahhhhh!" he cried as soon as he did.

"Stran, what is it?"

"Nothing, just a little wind burn," he said, trying to focus
past the pain and make his fingers work. "I just have to
make a few adjustments here."

One of the design changes was that the Cleanser had
been miniaturized. This device was half the size of the ones
Stran was familiar with. The advantage to that was that they
also had simpler controls. *Of course simpler isn't always
easier. Especially when you're trying to operate those controls with fingers that are having the epidermis flayed off.*
But with gloves on, there was too much risk of hitting the
wrong button, which could be disastrous.

Aeryn must have hit another updraft—or maybe it was
a downdraft this time—as Stran was thrown against the
bulkhead again. The bomb was still wedged into its place
under the seat, but Stran had to waste several precious microts clambering back to it.

Forty microts.

His fingers had gone red. Every time he flexed a finger,
pain wracked his entire hand.

Thirty-five microts.

Just one more . . .

Thirty microts.

He pushed the last button.

"Did it!"

Stran heard a long exhalation through his comm from

Aeryn. *"Good. Now get back in here so I can fly in a straight line for a change."*

"Happy to," Stran said, letting out a long breath of his own. He looked around for the gloves, but couldn't find them. Cursing at the pain in his hands, Stran activated the minijets and shot back over to the transport pod. They were safe.

Crichton sat in a corner of the Command with his recorder. He wasn't sure why he continued to record these messages to his father. He was able to recharge the recorder's batteries in *Farscape I*, but he was running out of tapes. Sooner or later, he'd have to record over the older messages, or just give up.

Maybe I should give up, he thought. *Stop fooling myself into thinking I'm going to go home again. It's like I told Aeryn, I'm completely cut off. No real chance of rescue. No real chance of getting the lyrics to "Viva Las Vegas." No real chance of ever seeing Dad again.*

He looked at Aeryn. *No, dammit. I'm not gonna give in to that. I won't.*

Pushing the PLAY and RECORD buttons, he started to dictate another note to his father.

"Hey, Dad. It's been a fun couple a days, but it's all over now. Zhaan's treating Stran's hands right now—he got a nasty case of windburn disarming that bomb. Good thing he was here—and a good thing Aeryn was able to talk him into helping." He considered that. "Probably wasn't that hard, really. I mean, it's his planet, too." He looked around the Command. "D'Argo and Chiana are off in a corner whispering sweet nothings into each other's ears. Rygel's still down on Liantac. When Zhaan's done with Stran, I'll take him down in the module—that'll show Ornara that my exhaust trick works, and then Buckwheat and I can finalize the deal and get out of here."

He smiled. "And it did work, Dad. It's my module that saved the day here. Right before I launched, you said you were proud of what I'd accomplished with *Farscape I*.

Well, now I accomplished something else with it. Hope you're proud of this, too.

"And we got a good deal out of it. Liantac is pretty much guaranteed as a safe haven for us. I don't think Aeryn or D'Argo or Zhaan'll want to come back here anytime soon, though Pip and Spanky'll be on the first transport pod down if we do come back. At the very least, it's good to know we've got a supply port. And maybe a source of information. I mean, it's possible that Ornara can find out about D'Argo's kid or tell us where Scorpy is."

Chuckling, Crichton continued, "Netoros didn't know as much as she thought. Crais's beacon only mentioned D'Argo, Zhaan, and Rygel, and Scorpy's only warm for my form, so Netoros didn't even know about Aeryn or Chiana. If she had, we might not have come out of this in such good shape. But we did, and I doubt Netoros or Garess will be able to do much of anything with the scandal they have to deal with. I certainly don't see the PKs coming back here any time soon. Ornara is arranging things so that the PKs get a report that Asmat died in a ferry crash." He chuckled. "If anyone bothers to investigate, Ornara said that all the witnesses who saw Aeryn impersonating Asmat were being tracked down and paid off." Another chuckle. "This place really *is* just like Vegas. Anyhow, Aeryn thinks the PKs'll still come eventually."

Looking over at Aeryn, who was leaning against one of Moya's consoles, Crichton added, "Speaking of Aeryn, she's got one of *those* looks on her face. Dunno how to describe it—it's kind of a life-sucks-but-I'm-dealing-with-it expression. She's been just staring at Stran since they got back from saving our asses. Part of me wants to talk to her about it—but I think we've done enough of that. It's always tough with her, figuring out how to get past the Peacekeeper officer and into Aeryn Sun. She's come a long way, but not as far as she wants." He bit his lower lip. "Or as I want, really. There's still a lot of the officer there."

Aeryn got up from the console and walked over to Stran and Zhaan. Crichton hit the STOP button.

Stran looked up at her.

"I just wanted to say thank you," Aeryn said haltingly.

Stran smiled. "What for? After all, it's *my* planet I saved."

"Not that—for trusting me. You had no reason to believe a word I said, and yet you trusted me with your life. I'm grateful for that."

Zhaan, who had been sitting next to Stran while applying some balm to his hands, got up. "That should do the trick," she said with one of her most gentle smiles. She handed Stran a small tube. "I wouldn't try to manipulate anything complex for a while, and apply this each morning for at least the next four solar days. You should be healed by then."

Returning her smile, Stran said, "Thank you."

"I just want you to know," Stran said after Zhaan left, "that I haven't forgotten what you did to me. But, in a way, I'm also grateful. There are a lot of things I miss about being a Peacekeeper, but I don't miss being one." Another smile. "Does that make sense?"

"Yes, it does," Aeryn said.

"Well," Stran said, standing up, "I'm ready to head back home. I didn't properly lock up the emporium when we left, so I need to get back and make sure that I haven't been looted."

"No problem," said Crichton. "Your limo awaits."

Stran frowned. "I beg your pardon?"

"Just ignore him," Aeryn said, "It's what we all do."

"It's all part of my vicious plot to confuse the galaxy and leave only chaos in my wake," Crichton deadpanned.

"And so far," Aeryn added, "he's doing a brilliant job."

Pilot chimed in. *"By the time you return, Commander Crichton, the Clorium field will have completely dissipated, and we will be able to leave orbit immediately."*

"Best news I've heard all day, Pilot." Crichton looked at Stran and indicated the door that led to the hangar. "This way."

As Stran followed him out of the Command, Crichton started singing a by-now-familiar tune, though he'd adapted the lyrics. "Viva Liantac. Vi-i-i-i-i-i-i-i-i-iva Liantac . . ."

ABOUT THE AUTHOR

Keith R. A. DeCandido grew up watching *Sesame Street* and *The Muppet Show*, corrupting him for life in such a way that he hopes never to recover. His other fiction has been created in the worlds of *Buffy the Vampire Slayer, Doctor Who, Magic: the Gathering*, Marvel Comics (Spider-Man, the Hulk, the Silver Surfer, and the X-Men), *Star Trek, Xena*, and *Young Hercules*. His most recent work includes a *Star Trek: The Next Generation* novel (*Diplomatic Implausibility*), a *Star Trek: Deep Space Nine* novel (*Demons of Air and Darkness*, coming in September 2001 as part of the "Gateways" crossover), a *Xena* short story, and a *Doctor Who* short story. Keith co-developed the *Star Trek: S.C.E.* franchise of eBooks, and has written or co- written five books in the series. Keith is also an editor, book packager, and musician—the latter with the acclaimed rock/blues/country band the Don't Quit Your Day Job Players (www.dqydjp.com). Learn everything you ever wanted to know about Keith but were afraid to ask at www.DeCandido.net.